"MAKE UP YOUR OWN MINDS. . . ."

"I want to tell you," Harrison said, "about the ways a man here in Goldfield might have his claim ripped away from him and from those he holds de... About how even after a man's de.... he could be robbed and the folks he loves denied what he worked to leave them.

"And I want to tell you where the truth of it all lies. So you boys can go see for yourselves if I'm telling the truth or not.

"Then I want you to make up your own minds about what ought to be done with a man who'd do that kind of thing to someone who called him a friend."

Ralph Horst grabbed at Harrison's feet and yanked at them, spilling Harrison off the tall bar to the sawdust and cigar butt–littered floor.

Horst began to kick Harrison's barely healing ribs.

Also by Frank Roderus
Published by Ballantine Books:

LEAVING KANSAS

REACHING COLORADO

FINDING NEVADA

Frank Roderus

Dave Lane
Tonopah, Nevada
March 22, 1992

BALLANTINE BOOKS · NEW YORK

Library of Congress Catalog Card Number: 84-28716

ISBN 0-345-32513-3

This edition published by arrangement with Doubleday and Company, Inc.

Manufactured in the United States of America

First Ballantine Books Edition: July 1986

For Bill and Merrilee Diers

"Funny, but all the things I used to be so positive about . . . the older I get, the less sure I seem to be of them."

—*Harrison Wilke*

CHAPTER 1

Harrison counted the scant handful of coins twice before he wrote down the amount on a deposit slip and entered the amount also in the passbook. He returned the passbook to the woman in front of his window with a smile and a nod. "A good week, eh, Mrs. Beamon? You're getting a tidy sum built up there."

She accepted it as a compliment and smiled back at him. "Thank you, Mr. Wilke. I shall see you again next week."

"Yes, ma'am." Mrs. Beamon—if there was a Mr. Beamon, Harrison had never seen the man inside the bank—came in to make her deposit regularly each week, on Thursday morning between ten and eleven o'clock without fail. This week's deposit had been $1.15, although sometimes she was able to save no more than the fifteen cents. But always she came into the bank to present her passbook and her weekly deposit. She had just over $65 in her savings account now, and it was money she had worked hard to accumulate. Harrison understood her pride of accomplishment and never failed to compliment her.

The work-worn, aging woman took her time about carefully tucking her passbook back into her handbag. Harrison smiled at her again when she was finally ready to turn away from the window. "You have a good week now, Mrs. Beamon."

"Thank you, Mr. Wilke."

She left the bank and Harrison busied himself with placing the coins into the cash drawer under the counter and making sure the deposit slip was correctly filed. He took pride in making sure that his drawer and his accounts were always in balance. The Miners and Mercantile Bank of Denver was no slovenly operation, and Harrison was always willing to give them his very best efforts.

A well-dressed gentleman, very young, came in and

looked around uncertainly. A new account, possibly, or a loan applicant, Harrison thought. Harrison did not know all of the bank's customers, perhaps, but he knew most of them. He was sure he had not seen this young man before. The young man looked about and turned to his left, toward the bank officers' cubicles instead of coming to the teller windows. Harrison let him go. Mrs. Hoeffner would be able to direct him adequately.

Young Mrs. Francis came in, and Harrison blinked. It would have been nice if he could think of some excuse to leave his station now. But that would hardly be fair to whoever would have to replace him and take care of Young Mrs. Francis's needs.

Within the bank—but certainly not outside it—Young Mrs. Francis was clearly differentiated from the previous Mrs. Francis.

Harrison sighed.

Certainly Charles M. Francis's very young bride had every right to do whatever she pleased with her own accounts. But every time C. M. Francis—who could hardly be considered young any longer—raised a question or an objection, the bride insisted that the bank was in error about the state of her sloppily kept and often-used accounts. At times she became quite argumentative about the alleged banking errors. No one in the bank enjoyed waiting on her.

And this morning it did seem that she had that look in her eye, ready for a fight, as she marched chin-high toward Harrison's window.

He arranged a smile on his face regardless. Every patron was entitled to that.

"Mr. Wilke."

"Yes, sir."

"Close your drawer if you would, please, and come into the office for a moment."

"Yes, sir." Harrison felt a distinct sense of relief when he placed the "Closed" sign at his window. Young Mrs. Francis angled away toward Anthony Kruger's window instead. Harrison supposed he should have felt sorry for Anthony, but he was more glad for himself than he was unhappy for Kruger.

He locked his cash drawer, tucked the brass-fobbed key back into his vest and followed the bank president into the offices, past Mrs. Hoeffner in the tiny reception area and into the sanctum with the ornate brass plaque on the door reading "M. Thomas Blakemon." Harrison never had learned what the M. stood for, even though in all likelihood he and Blakemon would eventually have a personal as well as a business relationship.

The young gentleman Harrison had just seen in the lobby was seated in front of Blakemon's desk. The young man stood when Harrison came into the office. Seen at this nearer distance, he seemed younger and a shade less well dressed than he had first appeared.

Blakemon performed the brief introductions. The young man was identified as a Harry T. Cole of Cole and Winslow, Attorneys at Law.

"Mr. Cole has some news for you, Mr. Wilke." Away from the bank the relationship was such that Blakemon called Harrison by his first name, and Harrison was permitted—but rarely felt comfortable in doing so—to call his employer Thomas. During working hours, however, formal address was always used. "I thought you would like some privacy," the bank president said.

Blakemon nodded to Cole and left, pulling the office door closed behind him.

"Yes?" Harrison asked.

"You are, uh, Harrison Wilke? Formerly of"—he looked puzzled—"The Rods?"

Harrison smiled. He began to wonder if this was some sort of elaborate joke. Certainly he could think of only one person who would identify him in that manner. "Yes, I am."

"Please sit down, Mr. Wilke."

Harrison was still smiling. There was only one chair in front of Mr. Blakemon's desk, and he would not have been comfortable sitting *at* the president's desk. Someday, possibly, but certainly not now. At Cole's urging, Harrison took the one available chair. He still suspected that there was some sort of foolery afoot here.

Cole struck a pose in front of him, hands clasped behind

his back in what he probably thought was a most lawyer-like posture. Harrison wondered if this young man might actually be a dramatist hired to play out a role here. Harrison tried to hide the amusement he felt and play along with it, whatever this was.

"My firm," Cole was saying, "has been contacted by a Horace Beechum, attorney, of Tonopah, Nevada."

Harrison found it truly difficult to hide his smile now. The name Tonopah was quite as much of a tip-off as that silly business about The Rods had been.

"Mr. Beechum has asked us to locate you and convey to you certain papers and requests pertaining to the estate of a John James Trohoe, with whom I believe you were acquainted."

Harrison was not smiling now. He felt cold. This *was* a joke, was it not? Please, he asked. Let this be a joke.

"I am sorry to bring you these tidings, Mr. Wilke," Cole was saying, "but apparently you are the sole beneficiary in the last will and testament left by the late Mr. Trohoe."

Harrison was barely aware of what else the young lawyer was saying. There was something about property. A mine. Something else about a house and some rather complicated wording about all goods, chattels and possessions.

The thing was . . . Harrison blinked rapidly. The thing was . . . John J. was dead. The best friend Harrison had ever had or likely ever would have.

And at . . . what? Harrison tried to think. He himself was thirty-five now. John J. had been fourteen years older. Dead at a vigorous forty-nine? It hardly seemed possible.

This was just some silly kind of a joke, right? Please, God, he thought, this just has to be a joke.

But that damned Cole just kept talking, droning on about wills and estates and nonsense like that. As if Harrison cared a fig about any of that.

No, this had to be some kind of morbid jest. And if Harrison waited long enough and patiently enough, eventually Cole would get to the punch line, and then Harrison could laugh.

Laugh until he cried.

CHAPTER 2

Harrison sat in the small room he rented. He sat in the single straight-backed chair that was provided for his supposed comfort. The chair was not particularly comfortable and neither was the narrow, lumpy bed. But the room was more than good enough for his needs.

It was, in fact, far, far better than the accommodations he had shared with John J. for all the years they had been together.

Harrison sighed.

All that time.

What had it been? Six years. Closer to seven. On the road together. On the bum, really.

Riding the rods or finding refuge in a boxcar when they could. Walking when they had to. That was what John J. had meant when he put that into his will. Harrison Wilke, formerly of The Rods. It had not been a place, like that young lawyer had thought. It had been a way of life. And John J. was the one who taught Harrison how to live that life, how to survive, how to pick up work here or a handout there. But a great deal more than simple survival. Oh, John J. had taught him more than just that.

Harrison smiled, in spite of the way he felt.

All those long years ago, back when they first met, back when John J. actually saved Harrison's life and then compounded the favor by taking him under his own experienced wing, Harrison had been—it was easy to admit now, although he had not been able to see it then—a shallow, pretentious, impossible little prig. So sure of his own superiority that he never looked to see what others had to offer, except perhaps what others *had*. In completely material terms.

That was one of the things John J. had taught him without ever once actually saying a word about it. It was more like something John J. had *showed* him during all those years on the bum.

Harrison smiled again.

Those had been good times, he realized now. And in truth, for much of that time he had even realized then how good the times were. Footloose and easygoing. No possessions, but no responsibilities either. *Free.*

Nearly seven years on the rods, and at the end of that time all of Harrison's pretentions, his snobbishness, had been left long behind.

Harrison owed a massive debt to John J. for that.

The man had taught him so much.

And in the end, oddly, it had been John J. who felt the urge to settle first. Harrison had always thought that he would be the one to decide to come off the road and make a place for himself in the "normal" world.

Instead it had been John J.

It had been a lady friend who put that bug in John J.'s ear, making him want to settle in and make something of himself.

Harrison still thought it was a shame that it had not worked out for John J. and Alicia. Not in the long run it hadn't.

But by then John J. had taken up a mining claim at Tonopah and built himself a house and was working harder than Harrison would ever have expected him to. And when the courtship went sour, as John J. had eventually written to explain to Harrison, old John J. discovered that he *liked* being where he was, doing what he was doing. So he stayed on and apparently had become a respectable member of the community over there.

Harrison still found that to be almost incredible.

Harrison sighed again, remembering.

For a while after John J. filed his claim, Harrison had stayed on, helping him open a shaft and build a waterless rocker/sifter to separate flakes of gold from the pulverized ore they took out of the mine.

But the work had been hard and, harder to take, the confinement to one place and one job had seemed strange after so long on the bum, and when it looked like John J.

6

had things running well enough for one man to handle the load, Harrison had drifted on.

He had never said so, but probably John J. had understood that Harrison felt awkward being in the way when John J. was trying to court that pretty grass widow too.

So Harrison had gone back to the rods and the freedom.

That had not lasted very long, though. Without the good humor and the companionship of his best friend, the road had not been the same.

Harrison probably would have gone back to Nevada and worked once again side by side with John J., but at the time it had looked like there would be a marriage soon and Harrison would not have wanted to burden his friend with another mouth to feed from that one, small-pay mine.

So he drifted into Denver after going back to Colorado to visit old Anson Freeman, another man who had taught him much in his youth, and now Harrison was a respected and rising young employee in the Miners and Mercantile Bank.

Harrison smiled. At himself. Ten years ago he would have thought the respectability of working in a bank was nearly the ultimate in what a gentleman could hope to achieve.

Now he thought that a position in a bank was a nice position for a man to have. He enjoyed the work and he enjoyed the people, and if the officers of the bank did not really understand that Harrison's popularity with the patrons came not from his efficiency but from his genuine liking for them, well, that was the bank's problem. Harrison did not truly care all that greatly how they perceived him. The fact was that he thoroughly enjoyed what he was doing.

He sighed again, wishing now that he had taken the time last year to travel back to Nevada for a visit with John J.

He had not seen his old friend in something like three years now. Oh, they had corresponded regularly. They were still the best of friends. But somehow, what with one thing and another, Harrison had never gotten back to Tonopah to visit John J., and John J. had never found the time to come to Denver.

Now it was too late.

And now that it was too late, Harrison was spending the afternoon berating himself for his failure to go for a visit while he still had had the chance.

CHAPTER 3

Harrison's quiet grief was interrupted by the sound of footsteps in the hall—the footsteps had the peculiar tock-a-tock cadence of a woman's walk, he thought—and a sharp rapping on his closed door.

He grimaced. The only woman who had ever visited him here was his landlady, and she was quite garrulous once she began a conversation. Harrison wanted to be alone now, not to launch himself into a conversation about unpaid bills—others', not his, as his own rent was always paid punctiliously and in advance—or the myriad other ills of operating a rooming house.

The visitor knocked again, and with a sigh Harrison rose. She must have seen him come in from the bank hours earlier than was usual. She must know he was in here. "Coming."

He opened the door. It was not locked. In all the time he had been using this room, more than a year now, he had never felt it necessary to lock his door and in truth did not know if the lock functioned.

"Martha," he said with obvious surprise. "I mean . . ." He glanced quickly down the hall to see if they were observed. It was not quite proper for him to address her by first name, even in private. It certainly would not be proper for her to be seen here, alone, at his bedroom.

Martha Blakemon ignored the ticklish social implications of her appearance and swept—that was the way Harrison thought of it when she moved, swept—into his room. Leaving him standing gaping at the open doorway. Swirling her skirts prettily as she turned and grasped both his hands.

"Dear, Harrison. Daddy told me your tragic news. I simply had to come offer you comfort." She leaned forward and pressed her cheek quickly against his, then turned her head just enough to give him a light buss on the cheek. She did not have to rise onto her toes to reach his cheek; she was quite as tall as he.

For that matter, Miss Blakemon might well have out-weighed Harrison by a few pounds. Not that he would ever have asked such an indelicate question.

Harrison had gained maturity over the years but not weight. He was still slender and wiry of build, although a touch of dignified gray had lately appeared at his temples and in the full mustache that was the custom for gentlemen to wear.

Martha Blakemon was as tall and had a full, buxom figure. *Zaftig,* some might express it. Certainly not fat. Had she been born into a different status she might have made an excellent artist's model for the type of paintings frequently displayed in drinking establishments. Her cheeks and lips were as full as her figure, and her face, high-lighted and dominated by bright, bright blue eyes, was surrounded by cunningly crafted ringlets of golden blond hair. At the moment she wore a blue velveteen dress suitable for daytime visiting or shopping and a matching bonnet trimmed with white lace. Strips of matching lace were sewn at the bodice and waist of her dress.

Harrison seated her in the one chair his room offered and glanced back at the door. He left it open so there could be no question of propriety. As there was no other place he might sit except on the edge of the bed, he was forced to remain standing. Both he and his guest would have to pretend that the bed was not present in the small room.

"Are you all right, dear Harrison?" Martha asked. Her face, really quite pretty with a touch of blush that might not have been completely natural high on her cheeks, was a mask of concern.

Harrison nodded.

"Daddy said the awful news was about the friend you have told us about so often," she persisted.

For one brief moment Harrison wished she would go away and leave him alone to think this out.

But that, he as quickly realized, was quite ungracious of him. Her concern for his feelings was genuine. She only

10

wanted to be with him in this time of grief. And she was probably right to be here. Perhaps the thing he most needed now was this assurance of caring.

Harrison nodded again. "It was John J." He shuddered. "Gone, they said. I don't know how."

"You have my sympathies, Harrison. Daddy's too, of course."

"It was kind of him to give me the afternoon off so I could be alone." After he spoke he hoped the comment would not be taken as a rebuke for her thoughtfulness in coming here. If she even noticed the wording she did not respond to it.

"He does care about you, Harrison. Almost as much as I do." She dropped her eyes from his and affected a faint blush.

Their relationship was understood if as yet unspoken. They had been keeping company for the better part of a year now. Sometime this fall, during the season of the galas that would follow the gentry's return from summer trips and excursions to spas in the cool mountains, their engagement would be formally announced. The period of engagement would last a minimum of a year. Neither of them had yet openly discussed the arrangement, but passing allusions and brief plannings made it clear that Martha would prefer to have the question asked and answer given within a few weeks prior to the All Hallows' Costume Gala in late October.

Throughout, the courtship had been conducted with circumspection and within the bounds of convention. Family dinners, picnics beside lakes and mountain streams, more recently at balls and ice-cream socials. By now it was expected that following family dinner invitations, the elder Blakemons would retire early and leave the "young people" to the privacy of the parlor, although with a maid in close attendance.

Oddly, under these unpleasant circumstances, looking at Martha while she visited his room for the first and quite probably last time, Harrison wondered how old she was. Twenty-two or -three, he guessed. Hardly of an age to be considered approaching spinsterhood but old enough to have to soon choose between that and marriage. He considered it his good fortune to have been found acceptable by her and by her family.

When Harrison did not respond to her comment—he did not know quite what to say to it at the moment—Martha raised her eyes to meet his again and coughed delicately into a gloved hand.

"Have you considered, dear Harrison, that you may well be a wealthy man now? I mean, the tragedy of your friend's passing is quite *awful*, dear, but he *was* terribly generous with you. In his will, I mean. And it is no great secret that Daddy has been counting on you to accept an appointment to management. Have you thought yet, dear Harrison, that you might wish to buy a partnership as well?" She was unable to conceal the pleased anticipation that sparkled in her blue, blue eyes.

"I hadn't really thought about that," Harrison said truthfully.

"Of course not, dear. Forgive me for bringing it up at this tragic hour." That was not really a question. It was a convention. There was no question at all that she fully expected—indeed probably felt there was no need for—the forgiveness she requested.

Harrison, however, was not thinking at the moment in terms of forgiveness for Martha or the possible wealth that John J.'s estate might bring him. At the moment he was still in a state of mild shock over the news the young lawyer had brought him.

CHAPTER 4

The Blakemon carriage took them to a narrow, stone-fronted building on Sheridan about two blocks too far off Colfax to be fashionable. It was the address young Harry T. Cole had given to Harrison the day before.

One day, Harrison reflected. It seemed longer. But at least now he had been able to accept that John J. was gone. The knowledge still hurt, but he was able to accept it.

Harrison waited for the Blakemon driver—who doubled as their grounds keeper and handyman at the residence—to climb down and move the collapsible step into place below the carriage door. Then Harrison left the coach and helped Martha to the sidewalk.

The driver closed the door smartly and nodded to Miss Blakemon. He gave Harrison a wink.

"Thanks, Charlie," Harrison said.

"Sure thing, Mr. Wilke. Should I wait?"

"Please."

Martha placed her gloved fingertips at the crook of Harrison's arm and allowed him to lead her up a short flight of steps that were grimy with coal soot and into a small vestibule.

A signboard indicated that the offices of Cole and Winslow were on the second floor. Harrison took the stairs slowly, conscious of Martha at his elbow. He felt slightly uncomfortable with her here, although her intention was to assist him through his period of difficulty. He did wish, though, that she had not affected a black dress today. She looked very much as if she were in mourning, the severe lines of the dress only partially relieved by a touch of lace at her throat and wrists and by the rose-cream cameo she wore at her throat. Martha had never met John J. and had expressed little interest in the friendship when he was alive.

Harrison had dressed as if for a day at the bank, in his usual suit of middling quality with matching trousers and vest but certainly with no armband or other outward display of his grief. He considered that to be a private matter not to be shared with strangers.

The offices shared by Cole and Winslow were spacious enough but consisted of a single room with desks, file cabinets and chairs arranged to give an impression of different office areas. There was no receptionist or clerk visible when Harrison and Martha entered, nor was there any sign of Winslow. Harry Cole was behind a desk in the far right corner of the room. He looked up when they entered and quickly shoved whatever he had been working on into a desk drawer out of sight. He stood to greet them, his welcoming smile dissolving quickly into a look of solemn sorrow as he apparently remembered Harrison's business here.

Harrison introduced Martha, and Cole fetched a chair for her. Harrison borrowed one from another desk and pulled it over so he could sit also.

"What may I do for you, Mr. Wilke?" Cole asked.

"Yesterday you said something about . . ."

"Of course. Of course. The particulars," Cole rambled while he pulled open first one desk drawer and then another in search of some papers. He produced them finally, in an envelope that showed indications of difficult travel, and handed them to Harrison. Martha leaned closer and looked on while Harrison shuffled through them.

"There isn't much, I am afraid," Cole said. "Very little to go on there, very little elaboration. Not at all the way things should be done, of course. All personal properties, to include a mine and a house. No inventory, however. None at all."

"No statement of estate value?" Martha asked.

"I am sorry," Cole said. "None."

"There should be an estimate of the value, shouldn't there?" she asked.

Cole spread his hands in unspoken apology. "I assume

14

the temporary trustee had not had time to complete such details," he said. "You will note that the, um, date of, uh, passing is quite recent."

Harrison read the cover letter addressed to Cole and Winslow. John J. had died on a Monday, little more than two weeks earlier. The letter had been written on Wednesday. That was something Harrison had forgotten to ask yesterday.

He tried to think back about what he had been doing that Monday. He could not remember. Not really. Nothing out of the ordinary, he was sure of that. He rarely did anything out of the ordinary any longer.

He smiled to himself a little, remembering. Come to think of it, he decided, he never had done all that much that was out of the ordinary. It was just that when he and John J. had been on the road together, there had been extraordinary things accepted by them as the ordinary.

It was disturbing to realize, though, that all this time had passed when he was ignorant of John J.'s death, time when Harrison continued with his normal routines entirely unaware of the loss that had been experienced so far away. He sighed.

"I suggest," Martha was saying in that no-nonsense tone of voice normally reserved for shop clerks and porters, "that you communicate with the trustees immediately. Mr. Wilke shall require a strict accounting of the estate. At once, mind you. And possibly a sale of the real properties involved."

Cole raised an eyebrow and looked at Harrison.

"What? Oh." He had been thinking, not really paying attention to what was being said.

At the moment he did not especially want to pay attention to this conversation. The air in Cole's office was musty and close. He had not noticed that before. He thought he could feel the beginnings of a headache.

"Is that your preference, Mr. Wilke?" Cole asked. "An accounting and quick sale?"

"I haven't really thought about it, Mr. Cole. An accounting, certainly. As to a sale . . . that would be premature. Surely I don't have to decide that sort of thing immediately.''

"Not at all," Cole agreed.

They talked a little longer, but the Denver lawyer knew nothing more than had been in the envelope, and that was very little indeed.

When they parted Cole assured Harrison that he would write to the temporary trustee, a member of a law firm in Tonopah, immediately with Harrison's request for additional information.

"Shall I call you at the bank when I have more information for you, Mr. Wilke?" Cole asked.

Harrison nodded. "By messenger at the bank or by mail at my home address,'' he said. A growing number of businesses and indeed some private individuals as well were subscribers to the telephone exchanged, but the officers of the Miners and Mercantile Bank of Denver thus far found it neither necessary nor fiscally prudent to adopt that particular innovation.

"Why did you tell that man to wait about the sale inquiries?" Martha asked when they were again seated in the carriage and Charles was taking them back to the bank.

"I haven't had time to think about it. Just like I told him," Harrison said. "That's all."

"Of course you haven't, dear. It was silly of me to bring it up so soon. But you must think it through eventually. This could be quite an opportunity for you, Harrison. For both of us, if I may be so bold. There is the possibility of a partnership. I mentioned that to daddy last night at table.'' Her voice sounded faintly British, and Harrison was reminded of the circles she moved within. There were a good many British gentlemen and their ladies in Wyoming and northern Colorado, investors and remittance men alike, and Martha and her friends seemed to have become acquainted with most of them. Nowadays a dinner party that did not include at least one member of the peerage was almost a disaster from the outset.

"And I was thinking also," Martha went on, "that you may be in a position as well to purchase a house. Nothing extravagant, mind. Something small but attractive and

16

. . . suitable.'' Her smile and the quick turning away of her head made it clear what purpose the house should be suited to. A first home for a young couple taking their place in society.

Harrison should have felt overjoyed by her openness. Instead he felt a stirring of mild annoyance. He simply was not up to this sort of discussion right now. Not yet.

"There is time to think about that later though, dear,'' Martha said quickly. She leaned forward in her seat and lightly touched the back of his hand.

Harrison nodded and closed his eyes. He wondered what he had been doing at the exact moment that John J. died.

The damned letter had not even said exactly how John J. died. Accidental death, whatever that meant.

It bothered Harrison that he did not know.

CHAPTER 5

For the next week Harrison went through the motions of his work and his everyday movements. Breakfast with the other boarders at the rooming house. An appearance at the bank two hours before the doors were opened to the public. Lunch bought from the vending cart that appeared on the street corner promptly at 11:15 each morning and remained there for an hour and ten minutes, the meal taken either on a nearby bench or at a desk, depending on current work load. A stop at the public library and one of several choices of cafes as part of the walk home each evening. Always the purchase of a *Post* from the solemn little Italian boy who each evening replaced the sandwich vendor on the street corner near the bank. Harrison had long since given up trying to tease the child into a smile.

At the best of times the routine was . . . peaceful. Quiet. That would have to be the most charitable way to put it, Harrison acknowledged. Boring might actually be more apt, he admitted.

Still, there were diversions and amusements.

Friday nights included a few drinks and perhaps a game of billiards at one of the establishments where the riffraff were discouraged. He did not enjoy card playing or gambling so avoided those invitations.

Later on each Friday night he would briefly visit one of the quieter, more reputable parlor houses. His visits were quick and uncomplicated, and he had never formed any particular attachment for any of the young women he had come into contact with there.

Saturday nights were quite, quite different.

On Saturday nights he generally accompanied Martha Blakemon to a recital or reading or perhaps to one of the magic-lantern exhibits that were still growing in popularity. They did not, however, dine together on Saturday evenings.

Dining was done in a family setting with the elder Blakemons in attendance, usually in the Blakemon home, less often in a public restaurant.

Saturday midday was generally the most satisfying period of Harrison's week.

Saturday mornings, although the bank was closed to the public, Harrison was among those required to participate in the detail work of close accounting and interest computation behind the closed blinds of the Miners and Mercantile.

After that, though, he would leave the other employees to their own private pursuits and walk not back toward his rented room but out toward the stockyards. If it was a foul day he would take a trolley; otherwise he would walk.

The stockyards were a sprawling, noisy, noxious area that straddled the railroad tracks leading northeast toward the Union Pacific main line.

The sounds and the scents were as familiar to Harrison as the remembered activities of a boyhood home. During the years when he and John J. had traveled together he had spent countless hours in similar settings. The flow of activity in and out of any town's stockyard makes it impossible for railroad bullies to know who belongs and who does not, so the stockyard had always been a favorite place to hop a rod or cop a lunch pail or even, in extremity, to look for a few hours of work.

Usually Harrison ignored the stockyards themselves, however. Usually he came here for other purposes. On this weekend, though, he paused to remember and was very nearly overcome with regretful nostalgia.

He shook his head and went on.

As with most such areas, Denver's stockyards were surrounded by a tenderloin district inhabited by the disreputable, the impoverished and the unwashed. The tenderloin included saloons and cribs and flophouses. It was to one of the flophouses that Harrison went every Saturday after the conclusion of business.

Martha Blakemon had never been able to understand why Harrison was chronically without funds. Harrison did

19

not know himself why he had never explained to her that this run-down building, identified only by a signboard reading BEDS 25c, WI EATS 35c, was the reason he so rarely had any cash to spare.

He walked into the downstairs foyer of the deep, narrow building and was surrounded by the odors of stale sweat, tobacco smoke and cabbage.

The proprietor of the place, a middle-aged man well along toward baldness, bobbed his head and smiled at Harrison's appearance.

"G'day, Mr. Wilke."

"Hello, Mr. Sawyer."

"A fine day it must be. I see by the time that you've avoided the cars."

"A fine day it is, Mr. Sawyer."

"Will you be taking lunch with us today, Mr. Wilke?"

Harrison smiled. "I don't know, Mr. Sawyer. Can I afford a lunch this week?"

Sawyer chuckled. "Per'aps the lunch should be on me this week, Mr. Wilke."

"That bad, is it?"

Sawyer shrugged. "They've started early this year. Down already from Montana an' the Dakotas. Must be a bad winter a-coming."

Harrison laughed. "I've heard people say you should watch the woolly caterpillar to judge a hard winter coming. The boys from up in the mountains swear you can tell it by when the elk and the deer leave the high pastures. I don't believe I have ever heard anyone advocate watching the movements of the road kings."

"Per'aps you should write an article for the papers on it then," Sawyer suggested.

"I'll consider that, Mr. Sawyer." Harrison pulled a leather snap purse from his coat pocket and opened it. Sawyer, observing, turned and began to rummage among slips of paper in a cigar box behind his counter.

"I have the figure here," he said. "Just a moment."

He found a scrap of paper showing a line of penciled tally marks, counted them and moved his lips as he tried to arrive at the calculation. After a moment he turned the

20

paper to face Harrison and pushed it across the counter. "You figure it up, Mr. Wilke. You're the one as can handle the ciphering."

Harrison glanced at the paper. There were two sets of five marks plus two more marks in an uncompleted set, a total of twelve marks. Ten of them at thirty-five cents would be $3.50, plus seventy cents would make a total of $4.20. He reached into the small purse for a $5.00 half eagle coin, one third of his weekly income, and handed the tiny coin to Sawyer. "You owe me eighty cents back, Mr. Sawyer."

Sawyer pulled out another cigar box, this one heavy with loose change, and counted out Harrison's money. Harrison put the coins into the purse, snapped it shut and returned it to his pocket.

Twelve this week. Nine last week. Normal was six or seven. Possibly Sawyer had something there about judging the severity of an approaching winter.

"You never answered me about the lunch, Mr. Wilke. My treat, mind."

"Thank you, Mr. Sawyer, but not this time, I think. I . . . have a lot on my mind today."

"Anything I can help with, Mr. Wilke?" There was genuine concern in Sawyer's voice.

"Nothing, but I thank you for the offer."

"If there is, you let me know of it, hear."

"I shall do that, Mr. Sawyer. Thank you."

Harrison turned and left, turning not back toward town as he usually did but wandering back in the direction of the stockyards. Thinking. Missing John J.

He was genuinely touched, though, by Sawyer's interest.

Sawyer was a good man and totally honest in spite of the circumstances that had placed him in such poor surroundings.

Handling the man's accounts at the bank, coming to know a little about him through that, had led Harrison to the arrangement they currently enjoyed.

Sawyer's business was not good and never would be in such a location.

And there were a great many men who passed through

the area who had no blanket, no food, no money to pay for meals and too little health or too little hope to take work.

So Harrison and George Sawyer had reached an agreement by which Sawyer would house and feed—for one night only—any hobo who came to his door. Harrison paid for their lodging and their breakfast.

Harrison was pleased with the arrangement. There had been times over the years when he and John J. had needed help. Now he was able to return that help to others who needed it. He considered his effort little more than a gesture, but it was one he was pleased to be able to make. The fact that his business also helped George Sawyer had quite honestly never occurred to Harrison.

He really did not know why he had never told Martha what he did with his salary. He was sure she would approve. After all, there was never a charity gala that she failed to attend. Somehow, though, circumstance and opportunity had never combined to make the discussion—confession?—seem appropriate.

Harrison walked to the tracks, smelling once again the coal soot and cinders and the warmer, richer odors of cattle and manure, and watched while a group of loud, laughing cowpunchers loaded beeves into a car.

He smiled thinly, remembering the time he had made the serious error of calling a cowboy a cow*puncher*. It had cost him three loose teeth—he had thought he would lose one of them but fortunately had not—to learn that a cowboy or cowhand considers himself above a cowpuncher, whose job it is to accompany cattle cars and make sure the beeves do not lie down where they might be trampled and killed.

The damage might have been worse that time if John J. had not been there to pull him away from the irate cowboys and convince them they should forgive his ignorance. As Harrison recalled it had taken John J. two or possibly three blows from that lean, wiry, deceptive strength of his to prove his point to the cowboys.

Harrison watched as a bull—the railroad, not the bovine kind—walked up and down the loading train, poking his

22

hickory baton between the iron car wheels to see if he might jab out a bo on the rods.

Harrison could not help but smile thinly at the performance. No bo worth his salt would allow himself to be caught that easily, and the fool bull was too fat and lazy to get down on his knees and *look*. Which was the only way he could expect to inspect those rods.

If anyone was under there, lounging on the hard rods while he waited for the train to move, Harrison wished him well.

After a time Harrison turned and began walking back toward the city. He needed to return to his room in time to wash and change clothes before evening. He was to meet Martha at eight this evening for a viola recital in a salon at the Brown Palace. For the first time that he could remember, though, he was not looking forward to the evening.

CHAPTER 6

"Of course you mustn't go alone, Harrison dear," Martha told him firmly. "Your emotional state is quite bad enough already. I wouldn't think of asking you to face this ordeal without me." She touched his wrist solicitously, obviously unconcerned that everyone in the bank was watching.

Actually, Harrison had thought his emotional state to be just fine, everything considered, but he did not feel inclined to debate that with her at the moment.

He wondered briefly how she had known of the summons from Cole. Then he realized. The young lawyer's messenger had reached him at the bank late yesterday afternoon. Information had finally been received from the attorneys in Nevada. Would Mr. Wilke please call at his earliest convenience.

It had already been too late to see Cole then, so Harrison had asked Blakemon for time off this afternoon. Obviously the man had mentioned that fact to his daughter.

And now Martha was here, dressed in one of her better city outfits and with the Blakemon carriage waiting outside, ready to accompany Harrison on another trip to Cole's office.

Harrison really would have preferred to go alone, but it would have been rude to refuse Martha's offer now. She seemed to be so concerned about him—much more, really, than he would have expected since the understandings between them were as yet unannounced. Not that those understandings were unknown. Anyone in their—in Martha's, actually—social circles was almost certainly aware of what was to come. But the fact remained, nothing had as yet been openly stated and therefore there were certain proprieties to be observed.

"All right," Harrison said. Barely in time to avoid an

embarrassing moment of awkwardness, he remembered to add, "Thank you."

Martha smiled and left him for a moment to sweep gaily into her father's office. Harrison closed and locked his cash drawer and pulled the short blind down over his window. By the time he had gotten his hat and umbrella from the rack at the back of the room and checked to ensure that his tie had not loosened, Martha was back in the lobby waiting for him.

"Daddy said we could take our time," she said. "You don't have to come back this afternoon if you don't wish."

Harrison did not have to ask whether Blakemon had offered the time or if Martha had asked for it.

"Anything new today?" he asked the Blakemon driver after he handed Martha into the carriage.

Charlie shook his head. "Not today, Mr. Wilke." He glanced aside quickly to make sure Miss Blakemon was not paying attention to them and gave Harrison a wink. "Want me to tip you if I get anything?"

Harrison laughed and shook his head. "Too dangerous for me."

Charlie waited for Harrison to enter the carriage and take the rear-facing seat across from her. He folded the step away and closed the door, then returned to the driving box.

Harrison doubted that Charlie Curtis would remain with the Blakemons much longer. Most of what Harrison knew about mining shares he had learned from Charlie, who bought and sold regularly in that volatile market. Harrison suspected that Curtis managed to do rather well in his dealings, if only because the man was so careful to avoid doing any of his banking at the Miners and Mercantile.

Harrison also doubted that it had ever occurred to M. Thomas Blakemon that Charlie Curtis did no banking with him. If anything, Harrison suspected, Blakemon would assume that Curtis did no banking, not that one of his employees banked with a competitor.

Charlie took them quickly to Cole's office building, and Harrison took Martha upstairs.

Harry Cole was not in at the moment. Instead they were

greeted by a man equally young and no more imposing than Cole, presumably his partner, Winslow. The man did not introduce himself.

"You are Mr., uh, Wilke then," he mumbled. He mispronounced it as Wilky, but Harrison did not bother to correct him. Winslow crossed the room to Cole's desk and rummaged in the papers there. "There was something, yes . . . here 'tis." He plucked an envelope from the papers and handed it to Harrison. He eyed Martha with too much approval—cheeky little bastard, Harrison thought—but did not offer them chairs.

"Harry said if you came by I should give you this," Winslow said. "If there's anything else we can do for you, let us know. I believe you will find our fees to be reasonable."

Martha sniffed once and turned toward the door.

"Thanks," Harrison said and followed her. He had to hurry to reach the door in time to open it for her. Her expression was icy.

When they were halfway down the stairs she said, "We shall have our own attorneys arrange the sale, dear."

Harrison refrained from mentioning that there was not yet a sale to arrange.

He waited until they were seated in the carriage before he opened the envelope Winslow had given him. He was barely aware of hearing Martha tell Charlie to take them to The Russian, which was a verbal shorthand for the name of a currently popular tearoom near the Brown Palace.

The letter, signed by a Horace Beechum, was brief:

Received yrs of the 12th inst, but I find it impossible to comply. Estate value cannot be estimated in light of the problems surrounding the claim dispute.

Please advise if you are prepared to defend title and whether fees will be guaranteed, if so by whom.

In addition to the letter, note really, there was a scrawled inventory list that began with "House on one lot, Tonopah" and continued with an interminable number of articles such as "Beds, two" and "Teaspoons, three" and "Desk, one."

Harrison read through it all, then handed the note and inventory list to Martha, who looked like she might develop eyestrain from trying to read upside down in the bouncing carriage.

"But Harrison," she exclaimed a moment later. "There is no mention here of the mine."

"Where it says 'claim dispute' I should think," he said.

"We must have this cleared up, Harrison. At once."

"I agree," Harrison said.

"The value . . ."

But Harrison was no longer paying any particular attention to her.

John J., he was thinking. His friend must have been having problems, perhaps deep and terrible problems, during his last days. And Harrison had known nothing about his friend's pain.

". . . Daddy's lawyers," Martha was saying.

"What?" Harrison asked. But he did not listen to her this time either.

CHAPTER 7

Martha was exceptionally pretty this evening, Harrison reflected as he moved carefully through the crowd of party-goers, balancing a cut-glass cup of fruit punch in each hand. She was wearing a gown of such a pale, pure rose that it looked almost white unless the light from the chandeliers was just so. And her hair was done in such an intricate mass of ringlets that it must have taken the entire Blakemon household the entire afternoon to arrange it. Harrison reminded himself, sternly, that he really should be more appreciative of Martha and of his own good fortune to be her escort.

He did not feel fortunate, though. And they had been politely arguing most of the evening.

At the far end of the crowded room the musicians had returned from their break, and he could hear the thin, plaintive sound of a single violin string under the bow as one of them tuned his instrument . . . or simply fooled with it. Harrison reached Martha's side and handed her one of the cups, then took a sip of the cloyingly sweet beverage. For a moment he rather envied the unattached younger men who had the freedom to spike their punch from the flasks they thought they were concealing inside their coats.

Martha accepted her punch with a smile, then frowned and returned to their earlier discussion without even tasting the drink.

"Really, Harrison, Daddy's attorneys can settle this whole thing. Truly they can. You shall have the best possible price for whatever Mr. Trohoe left to you, and then we can get on with our . . . with things here." She smiled, but weakly.

All evening long she had been telling him the same

28

thing, only her wording varying from one time to the next, and all evening long Harrison had been resisting.

It just did not seem . . . *right*. Turning John J.'s problems over to the impersonal hands of a group of lawyers just did not seem like the right thing to do. Although Harrison was not honestly sure what *would* be the right thing for him to do in this situation.

The orchestra was ready now, and Ronald Berrold interrupted the discussion by appearing in front of Martha to claim the dance she had promised. Martha checked her card to verify Berrold's claim, handed Harrison her still untouched cup and whirled away on Berrold's arm. Harrison did not bother to watch them. He turned away and went to lean against the handsome, flocked paper of the wall.

When Martha returned to his side, having to hunt for him to accomplish that, he returned the cup to her.

"I am going to Tonopah," he announced. The statement coming forth through his own lips surprised Harrison quite as much as it did Martha. He had not consciously thought it until that moment.

But once it was out he felt a sense of relief. It felt right to him. Much more right than remaining here amid the luxuries of Denver while his truest friend lay cold in a distant grave.

"Harrison! You can't be serious. What about your job? What about the partnership?"

Harrison shrugged. "Your father can give me a leave of absence or not. Whatever he pleases."

Martha looked at him closely. She must have seen the determination he felt now that the decision was finally reached, because her objections stopped immediately. "Whatever you think, dear." She smiled and touched his elbow, moving so she could stand closer at his side. "I am sure Daddy will give you a leave. An advance against your salary, too, so you can travel."

Harrison looked at her and for the first time in days crinkles of laughter gathered at the corners of his eyes. "I shan't need any travel expenses," he said. This, too, was something he had not thought of until this very moment.

"What?" Martha looked confused, as well she ought. She knew perfectly well that he had little money, however bright his prospects for the future.

Harrison chuckled and leaned forward with impish delight to kiss her lightly on the cheek, in full view of anyone who might have been watching. Martha blushed but looked pleased nonetheless.

"I shan't be needing travel expenses," he said, "because there will be no expense for my travel."

"But, Harrison . . ."

"I'm going back to see John J., Martha. I'll travel the way we always did."

"But . . ."

Harrison was feeling an odd excitement gathering low in his belly, threatening to disrupt his breathing, and now that a decision had been reached and openly stated, he felt a great sense of urgency as well.

Abruptly, rudely, he pulled away from Martha's touch, leaned forward again, but this time kissed her on the mouth. He was delighted by the look of pleased amazement that came into her eyes.

"Excuse me please, dear. Charles will take you home. Or ask Ronnie to ride with you if you prefer." He was already backing away, into the milling crowd of well-dressed guests.

"But, *Harrison* . . ."

He was smiling, and he looked quite boyish and impulsive. Martha had never, *ever* seen him look like that before. But then no one in Denver ever had.

He was gone before she could complete her protest, and she was left looking at her friends and equals assembled here for a gala evening.

CHAPTER 8

Harrison's heart was beating rapidly, a small thrill of the old, almost forgotten fear mingling with the pleasure of anticipation as he returned to the stockyard loading pens.

He thought he had accomplished everything he needed to. He had written a short note of apology—but not of explanation; he doubted that she would really understand an entire volume of explanation—to Martha. George Sawyer would post it for him.

His clothing and possessions—he had been startled to realize how few things there were after several years of living in one location—were also in Sawyer's hands. Oddly it had been the hotelkeeper to whom he turned when he needed that assistance. He had not felt all that close to any of his co-workers at the bank, and all of his social acquaintances were more Martha's friends than his; he would not have felt comfortable asking any of them for a kindness.

He probably could have retained his room or given it up and asked to store his bags in the rooming-house basement. But in years past he and John J. had too often lost what little they owned as the result of a landlord's impatience.

So he had chosen to pack his belongings and leave them and what money he thought he could afford with Sawyer. They should be safe enough there, he felt, regardless of how long or short a time he was away.

Now he was burdened only by the clothing he wore on his back. And none of that was fine.

He had on his oldest trousers and a suit coat that did not match, his oldest shoes and a shirt with neither collar nor tie attached. He wore a cloth cap for the first time in years, and among his pockets and shoes were distributed something like five dollars in silver.

He thought that he probably should have felt burdened

31

by this, particularly in comparison with the standards to which he had become accustomed in recent years, but he did not. In fact, he felt a twinge of guilt when he realized that he was no longer thinking about the loss of John J.; instead he felt an almost holiday like sense of gaity and excitement as he leaned against the rough wood of the stockyard pens and pretended not to be interested in the short freight that was being loaded.

A railroad bully came by, checking beneath the cars, and Harrison's eye lids tightened. He could feel old angers rising and old frustrations.

The man came closer and Harrison saw that it was only Marv Kraus.

Kraus was a loud-voiced, red-faced, happy sort who claimed to have once been a range detective for the Stockmen's Association in Wyoming and who now did his banking, what little there was of it, with the Miners and Mercantile.

Harrison knew him well, had known all along what Kraus did for a living. They had always gotten along well at the bank.

Yet now Marv Kraus was as close as Harrison had to an enemy. Certainly he was a person to be avoided at all cost today. Harrison tugged his cap lower and turned, slouching against the pen rails with his hands in his pockets, until Marv worked his way to the end of the train and passed around the caboose to the far side.

Today Marv Kraus was carrying a hickory club and might—or might not—have used it on Harrison's skull.

Harrison adjusted the set of his cap and took that opportunity to finger a bumpy ridge of old scar tissue above and behind his right ear. Marv Kraus had not put the scar there, but a man very much like him had.

Harrison waited until Kraus was several cars forward of the caboose—he could see the bull's feet moving beyond the open undercarriages, watched as Kraus stopped at each wheel truck—before he glanced up and down the length of the train and sauntered forward.

He acted as if he had no interest in what was going on around him, but that was a lie.

The cowpunchers who were loading the cattle he could ignore, but he had to be on the watch for train crewmen and for more of the hired bullyboys like Kraus.

He stopped near the chute leading up to the side of the car that was currently being loaded. The odors of manure and sweat and cinders were strong here but not unpleasant. The cowpunchers cursed and hooted, letting out shouts and shrill whistles to urge the unhappy cattle forward.

Harrison leaned against the side of the car, standing just forward of the back set of wheels, and watched for several minutes. His attention appeared to be on the cattle and the punchers, but in fact it was on the open area along the forward length of the train.

After a time he turned to check behind him. As far as he could see, no one was paying attention to him. Certainly the punchers were too busy to care what happened outside their chutes and pens.

Harrison smiled and knelt as if to tie a shoelace. He looked around one more time, then slid fluidly beneath the car and up onto the rods.

It had been a long, long time, but everything was exactly as he remembered, exactly as John J. had taught him. The cradle of steel rods, the dust, the heavy scents of grease and coal and . . . he wrinkled his nose in momentary distaste . . . of urine soaking through the floorboards of the car above.

The top of his cap was pressed against the wooden flooring of the car, and he wondered briefly when he might next be able to bathe.

Then, remembering, he laughed softly and felt tight muscles relax and accommodate themselves to the rigid surroundings. He was not bound by convention any longer. He did not have to take a room or find a barber's shop if he wanted to bathe. He could, in fact, wash himself whenever and wherever choice and opportunity commanded.

For the first time in a very long while, Harrison Wilke was once again among the freest of all free men.

CHAPTER 9

"Time. Out you go now. Everybody. Plates in the bucket, spoons in the pan. Everybody out." The jailer swung the door open and motioned impatiently. Harrison stood, joining half a dozen other men who had spent the night in the El Paso jail.

He quickly used a last scrap of cold biscuit to wipe up the final traces of lard gravy from the tin plate, dropped his plate and spoon where he was told and swallowed the bit of greasy biscuit without chewing or tasting it.

He let the other hobos file out of the cell before him and paused beside the guard. "Would it be too much trouble to let me borrow a razor before I leave?" he asked softly. He held his cap in his hands and was careful to avoid looking the guard in the eyes.

The jailer grunted once, then relaxed. "You're one o' them as came knocking, right?"

Harrison nodded.

"I expect it wouldn't hurt nothin'. End o' the hall then. Razor's on the shelf. Mind you don't use too much of the water."

Harrison nodded again and thanked the man profusely.

Last night's supper, a bed to sleep in, this morning's breakfast, now even an opportunity to shave the stubble that had been darkening his jaw ever since he left Denver . . . they were all comforts he owed to John J.

Once it would have frightened and shamed him to be found within the confinement of a jail cell. But John J. had taught him the value of seeking out the police and the jailers and asking for admission.

When a man is hungry, John J. had explained, it is better to ask to spend one night in a cell than to be caught stealing his meal and possibly spend a month of nights in the same accommodations.

It was something not all the bos were willing to do and something not all jails were willing to provide, but it was a handy thing to know and something he and John J. had resorted to frequently over the years.

Harrison smiled quietly to himself as he followed the jailer's directions, found what he needed and began to shave, making himself reasonably presentable once again. Once he would have approached the jailer with arrogance, even with disdain. And the man would have thrown him out, possibly with a fair degree of pain involved. But the simple expedient of holding his cap as a supplicant would and speaking softly and without eye contact had brought the fellow around, probably without him ever realizing that Harrison was working him, just the way John J. had taught him to do it.

Pride, Harrison reflected, comes in many guises. There was no pride in begging, but there could be a great deal of pride taken in a successful bending of a jailer's inclinations. He was still smiling when he finished his shave, pulled his cap down over his eyes and stepped out into the bright, morning sunshine with his belly full and his muscles loose after a night of good sleep.

Harrison paused for a moment to be sure of his balance, then hopped lightly over the coupling onto the frame of the next car forward. He swayed easily with the rocking, jolting motion of the cars and used his hands only occasionally for balance. He cat-walked out to the side of the car and used the side ladder for support while he swung around the corner and inched toward the open door he had spotted from several cars back. It would have been much easier to reach the door by going over the tops of the cars, but that would have risked exposure to anyone who might have been watching from the observation seat in the caboose. Better, he knew, to take the longer, slower route around or even under the cars than to be seen by a crewman.

He reached the doorway and stepped through into the shady interior of the car. He was not the first who had come to this comfortable sanctuary. There were already a pair of travelers reclining on a low stack of boxes near the back of the freight car.

"Howdy," Harrison said. He joined them, signaling his intention to stay a while—and therefore to remain in peace with them both—by removing his cap and dropping it onto the floor before he pulled a crate down from the pile of shipped goods in the car and placing it beside his cap for a chair.

The other hobos showed their acceptance of his company by moving their feet to give him floor space that he did not actually need. There had been more than ample room for him without their having to move.

"Hello yourself," the younger of the two men said. Neither was a kid any longer. The younger of them was probably in his forties, the other perhaps twenty years older. Both were in need of razors and tubs.

"There's a case of bully beef over here if you're hungry," the older man offered.

"I am. Thank you."

The one nearer the opened crate of tinned meat took out several cans and handed them to Harrison. Harrison nodded his thanks, opened one of the cans with the dull blade of his pocket knife and dropped the other inside his shirt for safekeeping. He used the blade of his knife—he had forgotten to bring one so had had to spend fifteen cents to buy one in Albuquerque—to eat his meal.

"Thanks," Harrison said again when he was done. He cleaned the blade of the knife on the side of his trousers and returned it to his pocket, then tossed the empty can out onto the roadbed.

"We're going to California," the younger man volunteered. "Going to pick fruit." He grinned. "They say it never gets cold there."

"Not as bad as most places," Harrison agreed. "Got any place in particular in mind?"

The hobo shook his head.

"If you get around Salinas try Carlton Farms. Ladder work, not stoop, and they treat you decent. At least they used to. It's been a while since I've been down that way."

"Is that where you're headed now?"

"Nope. Nevada. Mining country."

"I wouldn't want to work where I couldn't see the sun."

"Me neither."

The older man grunted and reached behind his neck to plump up the gunnysack bundle he was using for a pillow, then closed his eyes. "All the same to me," he mumbled. "Close to twenty year I been looking for a place I ain't seen yet. But they're all the same."

Harrison heard the crunch of gravel too late and entirely too close to let him get back beneath the car. The darn bull must have been able to sneak across a lawn of fallen leaves without making any noise. He was almost at the corner of the car before Harrison heard him.

Harrison spun around to face the coupling and began fumbling with the buttons of his fly.

"Hey! You!" the bull growled loudly. Harrison knew without looking that the ever-present club would be coming up ready for a vicious slash at his back or even at the back of his head.

Harrison turned, smiling, and managing to look sheepish and embarrassed. He finished fastening the top button of his fly and gave a little hitch with his knees, as if returning to a comfortable position.

"Sorry," he said pleasantly. "I didn't think I could make it all the way over to the outhouse so I slipped in here instead. There's some dang women on the platform."

The bull, a large man whose appearance would have let him pass for a hobo himself if it had not been for the bat in his hands, looked confused. "What?"

"I said I had to slip in here and take a leak," Harrison said. "I hope you don't mind."

"Oh."

"Excuse me," Harrison said, moving toward the bull.

The man backed up a step to let Harrison by.

Harrison walked out from between the cars, his shoe soles crunching loudly on the gravel of the roadbed. He put his hands in his pockets and strolled openly toward the depot building. There was a gold-lettered sign hung on the edge of the platform overhang. "Tonopah, Nev.," it read.

Harrison was whistling as he walked around the depot building rather than going inside it. There was no reason for him to enter. He had, after all, no baggage to claim there.

CHAPTER 10

Tonopah had grown since the last time Harrison was there. He would not say that it had matured particularly, but it had certainly grown. There were fewer tents now than there had been, the original flimsy structures replaced with wood and stone and brick. But even the brick buildings looked parched and sere in this dry, desert environment. Harrison's first impression was that there was no color in the town, neither in its buildings nor in the people he saw on the streets. Each seemed equally dry and dusty and monotoned.

There was certainly activity enough, though. Pedestrians and drays moved up and down the streets and the board sidewalks in a seemingly constant flow of motion, and the dust raised by feet and hoofs mingled with the smoke from coal-fired stoves to form a thin haze in an atmosphere that Harrison had remembered as being even clearer and cleaner than Denver's. The population of Tonopah must have quadrupled in the years he had been away, Harrison thought.

At least here his clothing would be no barrier. In Denver his rumpled, grease-stained, ill-matched clothes would have earned him suspicion at best. Here nearly everyone was dressed in rough, dirty cloth impregnated with grit the color of the rock underground.

Harrison's humor remained high despite the seriousness of the task that had brought him here. He whistled a cheerful ditty as he walked into town from the railroad depot. His good cheer earned him a wink and a bawdy invitation from an otherwise decorous-seeming young woman he passed on the street, but he went on by.

He asked directions of an aproned man sweeping the walk in front of a greengrocer's and was guided to a suite of offices on the second floor of a brick building. The ground level of the building housed a dry-goods store. The door leading to the upper level had gilt lettering advertising the services of H. Beechum, Attorney at Law.

Harrison climbed the narrow staircase to find offices that were not plush but which were certainly several cuts above those occupied by Cole and Winslow back in Denver.

Deep-seated, leather-upholstered chairs and a short sofa were provided for the comfort of the clientele, as were ashtrays, cuspidors and a selection of almost current periodicals from the East.

A young man, presumably a law clerk, had charge of the reception area. Harrison announced himself. He received a smile and a nod of recognition immediately.

"We had no idea you were coming, Mr. Wilke, or we would have arranged to meet you at the depot."

"My travel plans were uncertain," Harrison explained.

"Yes, sir." The clerk blinked twice and gave him an odd look but offered no comment. Harrison suspected that the man was remembering the business address to which the death message had been sent. Probably the poor fellow was having some difficulty making expectation accommodate itself to the reality that stood before him. Harrison smiled at him.

"Mr. Beechum is with a client now, sir, but I shall tell him you are waiting."

Harrison nodded and helped himself to a comfortable seat in the waiting area. He sorted through the newspapers and found a two-week-old copy of the San Francisco *Examiner*. The financial and mining pages of the newspaper were soiled from much handling, and Harrison added his own measure of grime to the page edges while he waited.

The clerk disappeared into a back office and returned quickly. A quarter hour later the young man rose to escort a rouged, overdressed woman out.

"Mr. Beechum can see you now, Mr. Wilke," he said politely.

Horace Beechum turned out to be plump, balding and much better dressed than anyone else Harrison had seen in Tonopah. He probably would have presented a hearty, distinguished bearing except for a poorly fitted set of false

40

teeth that clicked and whistled when he spoke. His smile of greeting was perhaps a shade too hearty and professional.

"Mr. Wilke. A pleasant surprise, sir." He reached across his desk to briefly shake hands, then motioned Harrison toward a chair. The chair was still warm, Harrison noted.

Almost before Harrison had time to settle himself, the clerk returned and handed Beechum a pair of brown envelopes, then let himself silently out again.

"I gather you have come to collect your inheritance, Mr. Wilke, although. we had been given to understand by, uh"—he checked a penciled note on the back of one of the envelopes—"by Mr. Cole that we would, uh, be handling a liquidation on your behalf. A liquidation, Mr. Wilke, is . . ."

"I know what a liquidation is, thank you."

"Of course, although many of our clients do not, Mr. Wilke." Beechum's eyebrows went up a notch. "Do I remember correctly that you are in banking, Mr. Wilke?"

"You do," Harrison agreed. He felt no particular compunction to offer the lawyer explanations about his choice of clothing at the moment.

"I see," Beechum said, although his expression and tone of voice stated just as clearly that he did not. "Now, sir, about the liquidation of the late Mr. Trohoe's assets . . ."

"Actually what I wanted to talk to you about, Mr. Beechum, was not a liquidation but an explanation. In your recent letter you mentioned something about a clouded title to the Rambling Bo."

Beechum looked confused. "The Rambling Bo, Mr. Wilke?"

"John J.'s mine. That's what he named it, isn't it?"

Beechum had to think for a moment, then he brightened. "Of course. The Rambling Bo. That was the title of the property Mr. Trohoe sold several months ago."

It was Harrison's turn to look confused.

"There was no difficulty with that title whatsoever, Mr. Wilke. I handled the transfer myself. A cash transaction, it was. Mr. Trohoe immediately reinvested the proceeds from

41

that property in a claim he refiled and titled the Amelia
One. That property, the Amelia One, is the property in
question here. And frankly, Mr. Wilke, I suspect there is
little or no likelihood that you could now recover title to
the Amelia One. You do, of course, have immediate possession of the property here in Tonopah, which would in
clude Mr. Trohoe's dwelling and all contents thereof." He
opened one of the envelopes and dumped a key into his
palm. He handed it across the desk to Harrison.

"But . . ."

Harrison was not sure what he wanted to say next. This
was not making a great deal of sense to him.

CHAPTER 11

Harrison turned the key in the lock with some difficulty, then pushed the door open and stepped inside. The house was little changed from the way he remembered it when he had been here before, but it had a different feel now. The heat inside the long-closed little place was stifling, and the air smelled dank and musty.

Harrison slipped the key back into his pocket and left the door standing open while he mechanically went from window to window, unlatching them and shoving them open to get some fresh air into the place.

He felt strange here, almost like an intruder in his best friend's home, but his thoughts were not on the problems of the house at the moment. At the moment he was thinking about what Beechum had told him.

According to the lawyer, John J. had purchased the Amelia One some time ago. And almost certainly he had been contemplating the sale of the Rambling Bo and the purchase of the other mine for some time before the transactions were completed.

Yet John J. had never once written to Harrison about any of it.

More amazing, the Amelia One was not even in Tonopah. Harrison was still a little unclear about just where the town of Goldfield was supposed to be except that it was not too far.

When Harrison was here before there had been no Goldfield, he was sure.

And now it seemed that John J. had had business dealings there. But never told Harrison about it.

Harrison could not understand that. He was, thank goodness, a little clearer now on what the problem of the mine ownership was supposed to be.

According to Beechum, John J. had properly and legally

sold the Rambling Bo, then properly and legally purchased the Amelia One in this Goldfield place. All of that was quite clear.

What remained in doubt, according to Beechum, was the ownership of the Amelia One now.

According to the lawyer, who frankly did not seem inclined to question or to contest the claim, immediately after John J.'s death by accidental fall, a new "owner" had attempted to take possession of the Amelia One.

The new owner, actually a manager representing a group of California investors, had a quitclaim deed in his possession conveying title to the Amelia One. He stated that John J. had used the deed as part of a wager in a poker game shortly before his death, lost the hand and the deed and subsequently signed away ownership of the Amelia One. The change of ownership had not been recorded, presumably because John J. had died before legal recording of the change in ownership could be accomplished.

The title was now clouded, Beechum said, because a third party was disputing the new ownership. Beechum explained that he had not been retained to represent the third party, a Mrs. Constance Wiggin of Goldfield, and that as far as he knew the title remained clouded but in the nominal possession of the California investors.

Harrison's opinion after talking with the lawyer at some length was that Beechum's interests were aroused by his retainer fees and that as far as the Tonopah attorney was concerned the transfer of the house key, a copy of John J.'s will and the deed to the Tonopah house were enough to fulfill his obligations to a deceased client.

As for the title to the Amelia One and this Mrs. Wiggin, Harrison had no opinion.

He did know, however, that he was hungry. He went to the kitchen in search of any nonperishable items John J. might have left behind.

CHAPTER 12

Harrison felt ghoulish. Coming to this house should have been a joy. A month ago it would have been. Now, with John J. dead and buried—it occurred to Harrison that he had never thought to ask *where* his best friend was buried—the place felt cold and empty and silent. He felt like an intruder here even though his own hands had once helped John J. build the place.

Little had been changed since then. There were a few more articles of furniture, a few more utensils and things in the kitchen. But very little had really been changed.

Harrison ate his supper out of cans, one of tomatoes and one of pears. There was a scuttle of coal for the stove, but he did not feel up to that much effort or trouble. Without thought he sat at the same end of the table where he had always sat before. He ate quickly and without pleasure, uncomfortably conscious of the fact that John J. was not and never would be again in his accustomed place on the other side of the small, secondhand table. As soon as he finished he went back to the main room. The little house consisted only of the living room, kitchen and bedroom. None of the rooms seemed particularly inviting.

When he lighted a lamp in the living room he was aware that it had been John J.'s hand that filled the lamp with oil, that it had been John J. who put out the box of matches that Harrison was now using. He sighed.

A book would have been nice to help pass the time, but John J. had never been much of a reader. There was not even a newspaper or magazine in sight in the living room.

He went into the bedroom and lighted another lamp there. It was very much the same as he remembered. There were the two beds they had made . . . no, he realized. There was one of the beds they had fashioned from scraps of lumber. The other was no larger but it was better built, possibly even factory assembled. That one obviously would have been John J.'s. The other would have been kept for occasional company. For Harison if he had ever gotten around to keeping the frequent promise of a visit.

In the corner there was a board and dowel arrangement that still served as a wardrobe. John J.'s winter coat, sheepskin lined, hung on it. It was not a coat Harrison had ever seen before, but he knew without trying it on that the shoulders would be slightly too broad, the sleeves much too long for him.

A small desk had been added in the opposite corner with an ink bottle and set of steel-nibbed pens. There were no books in evidence, but there was a bundle of envelopes that Harrison thought he recognized.

He stepped closer and felt a pang of fresh sorrow when he examined the letters.

They were all familiar enough. They should have been. He had written each of them himself.

He shuffled through the stack from top to bottom. They seemed to all be there, every letter that Harrison had ever written. All had been saved. They were crumpled and looked like they had been much read. He had had no idea that John J. would have bothered to save them all.

Harrison had not saved the letters he had received from John J. over the past few years. There had been enough of them. Probably one to match each of these that John J. had preserved. Yet Harrison had read them, enjoyed them and then threw them away. That knowledge made him feel guilty now. Perhaps unworthy.

He blew the bedroom lamp out and left the room in dark silence. He could sleep on the sofa tonight. Tomorrow he would go to Goldfield and ask Mrs. Constance Wiggin why she was interested in the ownership of the Amelia One.

At least for the time being he did not even want to think about the chore of disposing of this house and the things John J. had put into it.

CHAPTER 13

"Thank you, sir."

"Anytime, young fellow. Glad to be of help."

Harrison hid a thin smile of puzzled amusement—and perhaps amazement as well—as he turned his back on the old gentleman to jump down off the wagon box. Young fellow, indeed. In his mid-thirties and gray at his temples, yet people still called him young fellow. He supposed it should be taken as a compliment of sorts. He supposed.

He thanked the man again and waved as the driver shook out his lines and picked the team up into a slow walk. Now that they had reached Goldfield—it was only a few hours from Tonopah—there was no more need for the sweating mules to hurry.

Goldfield was as raw now as Tonopah had been the last time Harrison was in this part of the country. Without doubt if Goldfield thrived and grew the way its slightly older sister city had, there would be a railroad here in another year or two. But for now there was only the dry, dusty wagon road. A much-traveled wagon road at that, Harrison noted. Commerce seemed busy, the infectious fever of precious metals drawing men, mules and material alike into the booming town.

The country around the strike, though, was little different from that around Tonopah. Dry, barren and hot, the land seemed malevolently determined to parch, pierce, choke or bruise whoever dared pass through it. Or so it seemed at the moment, even though Harrison knew better. The land, he realized, was merely indifferent, supremely indifferent, to any who entered it.

Besides, his concern here was not with vistas of beauty but with the questions of a confusing legacy.

He hefted his bag—he had taken the liberty, albeit uncomfortably, of borrowing clean smallclothes and a fresh

47

shirt from the trunk in John J.'s bedroom—and went in search of Mrs. Constance Wiggin.

The people who had come here, he quickly found, were so infused with enthusiasm for their own prospects that they were cheerful and friendly with strangers. The feeling seemed to be that one man's prospects were so fine that another's possible prosperity was neither threat nor obstacle and so they could be open and pleasant with all, with no restraint from competition or jealousy.

A stop at a saloon built half of stone and half of canvas gained him directions to a long, grimy tent that must once have been white but which now had taken on the grayish tan shades of the dust that rose from the street before it.

A hand-painted sign was nailed to the stout pole that supported the street-side end of the tent. EATS was the message. No prices or menu were included.

Harrison entered. The interior of the tent smelled of grease and fried foods and hot canvas, but the shade gave an impression—probably spurious—of coolness after the glare and the heat outdoors.

Two long tables had been crowded into the street end of the place, each with sturdy benches to accommodate the diners.

Beyond the tables and separating probably the rearward third of the tent from the public area, a canvas drape had been hung. Harrison assumed that the rearmost portion of the place was the kitchen.

A square of white cloth had been pinned to the draped canvas "wall" offering meals for thirty cents, sandwiches at ten cents or pie and coffee for ten cents. Harrison had no way to judge whether the rates were fair in this time and place, but the number of customers noisily seated at the tables made him suspect that either the rates were low or the food was exceptionally good here. Most of the benches were either full or nearly so.

Harrison felt of his pockets. He had a little cash left, and he was hungry. He squeezed onto the end of the nearest bench, and an obliging diner shifted sideways, taking a tin bowl of aromatic stew with him.

"Thanks," Harrison said.

The man grunted once and went back to his meal.

A young woman came through a slit in the back wall carrying a round tray. She delivered stew, bread and coffee to several men and gathered up the empty utensils from two or three more recently vacated seats before she noticed Harrison.

"Yes, sir?"

He got a better look at her when she turned to face him.

She was young, as he had already seen, but not as young as he had first thought. Somewhere in her twenties, he guessed now.

It was her size that had given him that first, false impression. She was not tall and was almost painfully thin.

She was plain, especially so since her hair was pulled back into a severe bun and her face was shiny with perspiration. She wore a dowdy gray dress and an apron that was stained with gravy and grease and other, less identifiable leavings from other people's meals.

Her eyes were nice, though, Harrison thought. A bright hazel with flecks of green and gold when the light hit them right. And he rather liked the impression of cheerfulness given by the laugh lines that radiated around both her eyes and the corners of her mouth.

Her cheekbones were a trifle high, her nose straight, lips full without being pouty.

Perhaps she was not quite as plain as he had first thought.

It occurred to him that he was paying entirely too much attention to what this woman looked like and entirely too little to the reasons he had come here. He looked quickly away from her and pretended to cough into his fist.

"Did you want something to eat, sir?" she asked.

"Yes, I . . . do you still have breakfast?" It was mid-morning and the stew smelled marvelous, but breakfasts are generally cheaper than lunches.

"Yes, sir, I think we still have some oatmeal left. No milk or cream for it, though. I could bring you that and coffee. Ten cents. Would that be all right?"

Harrison nodded. "I . . . are you Mrs. Wiggin?"

She had been about to turn away toward the kitchen, but

now she stopped. She cocked her head to the side—rather prettily, he thought—and paused for a moment. Then she smiled. "No, sir, Mrs. Wiggin is my mother."

"Could I have a word with her then?"

"She is terribly busy right now. Is there something I could help with?"

"I could wait," Harrison suggested.

"It might be after dinner before she has any time for you. But if you're trying to sell something . . ." She sounded doubtful about that, and Harrison was reminded of his present appearance. He hardly looked the part of a drummer. He smiled. He hardly looked like a banker either, for that matter.

"I can wait," he said.

"Yes, sir. I'll tell her you want to see her."

"Thanks."

The girl hurried off toward the back of the place, having to stop several times along the way to take orders or to gather empty bowls as she went.

CHAPTER 14

Mrs. Wiggin was an older version of her daughter. Small, slightly built, eyes and expressions pleasant. She had the same, sensible style of clothing and the same coloring. They might have been taken for sisters whose age was not unreasonably distant. She came into the dining area after the dinner crowd had thinned and there were only a very few diners lingering over their coffee. She carried a towel that she was using to dry her hands, while her daughter brought the inevitable coffeepot.

Harrison had become quite well acquainted with that pot during the past several hours. He had had to make several trips to the nearest privy while he waited, but the girl, whose name he had not asked, had not charged him any additional fee for the gallon or so of coffee he had consumed.

The girl refilled Harrison's cup yet again, then stepped back to wait beside and slightly behind her mother, who was giving Harrison a close inspection and not troubling to hide that critical assessment.

"Well," Mrs. Wiggin said after a moment, "you aren't another damn lawyer. Not dressed like that you aren't, though I daresay you might clean up to something half decent if you were of a mind to." She did not sound hostile. Exactly. But Harrison got the impression she was ready to get that way at any moment.

"No, ma'am," Harrison said. He laid his cap aside and stood. He did it awkwardly, having to keep his knees bent to avoid tipping over the bench that had been set rather too close to the table.

"Well?" Mrs. Wiggin demanded before he could add anything else.

"My name is Harrison Wilke, ma'am, and . . ."

He did not have time to explain any further. Mrs.

Wiggin looked shocked. She took a half step backward, her hand rising toward her throat.

The girl's reaction was equally puzzling. She squealed with immediate and obvious pleasure and stepped around her mother to grab Harrison's right hand in both of hers and cling to him.

"Harrison?" She was grinning broadly. "I mean . . . Mr. Wilke? Are you truly?"

"Why, yes, I . . ."

Mrs. Wiggin recovered her composure and stepped closer. She was smiling, too, now. She took Harrison's other hand. They did not seem to want to shake hands, nor were they leading him anywhere. Both women just seemed to want to touch him, perhaps to cling to him for a moment.

"Forgive us, please, Harrison." She amazed him all the more by rising on her tiptoes to give him a kiss on the cheek.

"Ma'am?" he stammered. "I don't understand."

She continued to smile. "You did come here about Johnny, didn't you?"

"Johnny?" Harrison could not remember when, if ever, before he had felt so completely stupid.

"You *are* Harrison Wilke of Denver, yes?"

He nodded.

"Although I daresay you look nothing like the bankers I have met in the past." She laughed and poked a finger at the dusty lapel of his coat.

Mrs. Wiggin turned to her daughter. "I don't believe dear Harrison knows what to make of us, Nevvie."

The girl laughed and moved nearer to take Harrison by the arm with a familiarity that was disconcerting at best. "What were you expecting, Harrison? What did Johnny tell you about us?"

"Johnny . . . ?" Harrison mumbled. It occurred to him finally that they had to be talking about John J., although never, ever had he heard John J. referred to as Johnny. Never.

"You did come to see us about Johnny, didn't you?" Mrs. Wiggin asked. But she sounded worried now.

"Yes, ma'am," Harrison conceded.

Mrs. Wiggin smiled again.

"We have to do something to celebrate tonight, Mama," the girl said. "This visit calls for something special."

Harrison was still confused. He was not entirely sure what these two odd women might be up to, but he allowed them to lead him toward the back of their cafe and through the canvas curtain into the kitchen, which turned out to also house their living quarters.

They were not wealthy, he thought. And Mrs. Wiggin was obviously making some kind of claim on the Amelia One, which would have been Harrison's property if the title had been clear.

They were up to *some*thing, he thought.

But what?

CHAPTER 15

The kitchen/sleeping portion of the tent was stifling hot from the heat radiating fiercely from the stove, even though the back and side walls had been rolled up for a distance of several feet from the earth floor.

The stove dominated the area. Against the opposite wall, exposed now to foot traffic outside, were two carefully made cots and several small trunks. Crates and boxes of foodstuffs were stacked at the back wall, and the center of the area held a massive butcher block. The girl pulled a stool next to the butcher block and motioned Harrison toward it while her mother brought him a fresh cup of coffee to replace the one he had just left in the public room.

"What can we do for you, Harrison?" Mrs. Wiggin asked. "Anything at all, just name it. You were Johnny's best and dearest friend and, forgive us, but it seems like we've known you ourselves for all the years that Johnny did." She smiled. "He talked of you almost constantly, you know."

"No, I didn't know," Harrison said lamely.

"He told us he wouldn't write you about the wedding," Mrs. Wiggin chattered as she went to the stove and began to fuss over something there.

"Wedding?"

"That was going to be a surprise. But you couldn't know about that, could you? We were going to go to Denver on our wedding trip. That was the surprise. He wanted to drop in on you." She laughed, her eyes becoming exceptionally bright. "It would have been quite a surprise, of course. And he used to become so gay when he planned for it. He said . . . he said it would be the first time he could remember actually *paying* a train fare."

She had been talking rapidly, faster and faster, her eyes

54

growing brighter as the words poured out. She turned and pointed toward a large can on top of one of the crates toward the back of the room. "Fetch me the cherries please, Nevvie. I think a cobbler would be nice tonight to celebrate Harrison's arrival, don't you? And perhaps a brisket baked in my brown-sugar sauce. Would you like that, Harrison? It was Johnny's favorite. It was the way we . . . the way we . . ."

Inexplicably, Mr. Wiggin burst into tears. She turned and started toward the public room, thought better of that and stood for a moment in indecision. Obviously she had no private place she could run to. After a moment she wiped her face with the hem of her apron, picked up a tray and walked quickly out into the public room.

The girl brought the can—it looked large enough to contain a gallon of the cherries in heavy syrup—to the butcher block and began to open it.

"I hope you understand, Harrison. It isn't your presence that upset her. I know Mama is as happy to see you as I am. It is just that . . . there are so many memories. Like Johnny's favorite foods. That is what she was about to say. It was because he liked her baked brisket so much that they met. And everything." She poured the syrup off the cherries into a bowl, got a device that looked like a metal plunger from a box and began using it to pit the cherries, transferring them one by one from the can into the bowl of syrup, her hands gracefully but mechanically busy as she talked.

"The wedding was supposed to be next week, you see," she was saying. "But you wouldn't know that either, would you? Johnny said the whole thing was supposed to be a surprise." The girl sighed. "How he was looking forward to seeing you. You simply can't imagine it. He couldn't have felt any more for you if you had been his own brother, you know. Or son. I don't believe Johnny knew himself which he thought of you as. But then you probably know all that."

Harrison nodded. He felt numb, dumfounded.

If these women were telling him the truth, John J. had

intended to marry Mrs. Wiggin. This very month. And to visit Harrison in Denver.

That *might* explain why John J. had not mentioned them to him. Or they might as easily be lying to him because of that still unexplained claim they had made against the Amelia One.

Yet even if John J. had chosen not to tell him about the wedding plans, Harrison thought, that did not explain why nothing had ever been said about the Amelia One and the sale of the Rambling Bo or about John J.'s change of mining interests from Tonopah to Goldfield. It explained nothing of that.

Then, too, why would John J. have not mentioned Mrs. Wiggin and her daughter? He could believe John J. might choose to keep the wedding a secret. But why the women themselves? Surely John J. would have told him if he were truly interested in a lady here. Certainly Harrison had written John J. everything about Martha, about the bank, about very nearly everything he had seen and done over the past few years, with the single exception of his dealings with Mr. Sawyer and the room and board for the traveling bos. Harrison would have been embarrassed to be found out about that; he had never mentioned any of that in his letters to John J.

"He did tell you about me, you say?" Harrison asked.

"Oh, goodness yes," the girl said. Harrison tried to remember what her mother had called her. Nevvie? He decided it would be safer to call her Miss Wiggin even though she was addressing him by first name. "All the time," she went on. She finished pitting the cherries and dumped them into a shallow baking pan, then began to mix a dough to put over them for the cobbler.

"Are you and Miss Blakemon formally engaged yet?"

"What?"

"No, of course not," the girl corrected herself. "Johnny said you wouldn't do that until this fall, wasn't it?"

"Uh, yes."

She began to beat the dough to mix it. She seemed to have a good deal of strength despite her small size. "I suppose I shouldn't be so forward, so personal on such short acquaintance, and all that," she said, "but it's a bad habit I have, I suppose from growing up in the mining towns where nearly everyone is a stranger anyway." She laughed. "I can't begin to remember all the times we've moved or even, probably, all the camps we've lived in."

"Was your, uh, father a mining man?"

She nodded. "Never a very successful one, though. Whatever he made he managed to lose. He liked to drink, you see. That was one of the things Mama found so dear about Johnny. Johnny never drank all that much. He said it gave him indigestion."

That was true enough, Harrison remembered. John J. enjoyed an occasional drink, but excess always gave him a sour stomach for days afterward.

"Am I talking too much, Harrison?"

Harrison shook his head.

"The truth is, I think, that I'm a bit nervous. I mean, it is *almost* like we know you. Because of Johnny. But . . . you are such a gentleman and everything. Johnny told us that too. He was so pleased when you found that job at the bank. He said you belonged in a position like that. Or in politics. He always thought you would make a wonderful politician."

That was certainly something that John J. had never indicated to Harrison, if it were true.

"He was so awfully proud of you, you know." She sighed. She ladled sugar and cornstarch over the cherries, then began to cover them with the dough she had made. "Mama and I haven't had much experience with gentlemen, you know. Not real ones, though I can remember Daddy admiring men who were new rich from their claims. Some of them were all right, but most really weren't. It was like their heads got all swelled up when they came into money. To tell you the truth, I think Daddy would have been like that if he had ever gotten rich. But Johnny always said you were the kind of man who was a gentleman with or without a cent in your pocket."

"Really?"

"Oh my yes. He said that I don't know how many times. He meant it too. I could tell."

She laughed. "He told us you almost weren't like that, that you were quite the proper mess when he found you, but that a gentleman named Freeman put you back on the right path."

Harrison conceded that John J. had had some serious discussions indeed with these women if he had gotten around to talking about ancient intimacies of that sort.

"He told us about that affair in Cripple Creek, you see. He made it sound like quite a lark, but I suppose it was dreadfully serious at the time."

"It was," Harrison agreed without elaboration. Although serious had only been the half of it. It had also been damned well embarrassing. He had felt like quite an ass when he realized that the money he thought he was protecting from robbers was money he had actually, if unknowingly, stolen from bonded courier guards. It had been in the midst of all that when John J. had come into his life with a helping hand.

"It sounded quite funny when Johnny told it," the girl said, "and it made an impression on me because Cripple Creek is one of the places I can remember living before Daddy died. We got there too late in the rush for Daddy to locate a claim, so he had to work for wages until we could get enough money together to come back to Nevada."

She finished smoothing the thick dough over the newly made cobbler and carried the pan to the oven. She put it inside and checked the firebox. "Just about right, I think," she said. "You want coals for baking. Too hot and you scorch the crust." She wiped her hands on her apron and looked worriedly toward the entrance to the public room. "I hope Mama is all right."

"I'm sorry if I upset her," Harrison said. "I could leave if you think . . ."

"No," she said quickly, "Please don't do that. It would just upset her that much more if she thought we hadn't made you welcome here. Don't you know, Harrison, that you are the last link she has with Johnny?"

Harrison settled back on the stool and took a sip of the

coffee he had been given. It was already too cool to be palatable, but he sipped at it anyway.

He was beginning to wonder how upsetting it would be for them if he just slipped quietly away.

CHAPTER 16

". . . and so," Harrison finished explaining, "I came here to see what the problem was with the title to the mine, although the truth is that I had a different mine in mind when I set out from Denver. I had no idea John J. had bought this Amelia One."

Mrs. Wiggin put another huge spoonful of cherry cobbler in Harrison's bowl and gently coughed. She seemed to be taking a moment to make up her mind about something.

"It won't do any harm to tell you now, of course," she said, "so perhaps I should explain why Johnny did not write to you about the move to Goldfield."

"Please." Harrison took another bite of the cobbler. He had already discovered that it would have been pointless to try to refuse Mrs. Wiggin's offers of food and attention.

"By the time he bought the Amelia One, Johnny and I had already been . . . seeing each other . . . for some time. We met when he was over here looking for a good location in this new camp. We became . . . close . . . very soon after we met. It was an instant love, if I may be so bold as to use that term. Although neither one of us had any such intention. We met, and almost at once everything seemed so . . . right. So natural. And almost that soon we planned an engagement.

"The suddenness of it was quite embarrassing in a way. But oh, so thrilling in another." She blushed. "It is an experience I never hoped nor certainly expected to have in my lifetime."

The conversation was becoming much more intimate than Harrison was really comfortable with, but Nevvie Wiggin acted like she accepted it as perfectly natural and normal to hear her mother speak of affections for a man who was not her father.

"Just as quickly, Johnny thought how much fun it would

60

be to surprise you. As soon as we began talking in terms of marriage, he spoke of his desire to take our wedding trip to Denver so you and I could meet. This was shortly after you had written to him about your, uh, intentions toward Miss Blakemon," she said.

Harrison tried to think back. If he remembered correctly, that would not have been so very many months ago. He had been seeing Martha for some time before they grew serious enough for him to write John J. about her.

"So he already had that surprise in mind. And then he began to worry too. About whether he should even tell you about the purchase of the new claim. At that time the Amelia One was virtually undeveloped. Just enough mineral had been taken out to establish legal requirements for the claim filing. Then Johnny bought the property."

She sighed. "He made a very nice profit on the Rambling Bo, you see, which was beginning to show signs of faltering production, and of course the production never had been all that great to begin with. I suppose you already knew that."

Harrison nodded. The inferior production quality of the Rambling Bo had been one of the reasons he had left Tonopah to begin with, and the ore body never had become much better than they had found for that initial filing. That was one of the things John J. had kept him fully informed about over the years, although Harrison had certainly never thought during any of that time that he would be named as John J.'s heir. John J., however, must have had something like that in mind for all this time yet never told Harrison about it.

"Anyway," Mrs. Wiggin continued, "he began to worry about what would happen if he told you he was starting this new venture in Goldfield. Frankly, Harrison, he was afraid you would feel that you should come out here and help him with the development work."

"Of course I would have," Harrison said. "If I'd had any idea that he needed me . . ."

"Exactly," Mrs. Wiggin said. "That is exactly what he thought you would feel. And he was *so* proud of your success in Denver. Johnny didn't want to say or do anything that might harm your career, you see."

Harrison bit his lip. He remembered some time ago, probably around the same time he had written to John J. about Martha, mentioning her father's interest in his prospects with the bank. And—he hated to admit it to himself, but it was the truth—bragging somewhat about the likelihood of a promotion to the head teller's office in the near future.

Damn! he thought. Would he never learn?

"We talked it over," Mrs. Wiggin said. "If you are angry with me, well, you have every right. We talked it over, and I agreed with Johnny that we should keep the whole thing a surprise. He could tell you both pieces of news when he saw you." Tears were welling in her eyes when she added, "We both were sure that that would be late next month, you see. We didn't think it would do any harm."

"I was going to stay here and keep the cafe open while they were gone," Nevvie added.

"We certainly never meant to cause you any distress," Mrs. Wiggin said. "But we certainly had only the best of intentions too. Are you angry?"

Harrison shook his head. Sad, yes. But not about anything related to any gold mine.

Being here, being in the places and with the people who had been the last part of John J.'s life, made Harrison miss his friend all the more.

"And I hope you don't mind that I filed a protest about the transfer of ownership of the Amelia One to those California people," Mrs. Wiggin added, broaching that question herself before Harrison eventually had to.

"Mama and I discussed that just after Johnny died," the girl said. "We knew, of course, that the property was supposed to be yours. So Mama filed that claim just to make sure the Amelia One would not be taken over and given to someone else just because you couldn't be here to protect your interests."

"What was the basis for your claim against it?" Harrison asked.

"To tell you the truth," Mrs. Wiggin said, "there really was no basis for it."

"We invented one," Nevvie said.

"When we filled out the paper we had to write something down."

"So we put down something about conflict of claimed ownership."

"We didn't have to specify at that time what the conflict was, you see."

"We just had to say that there was one."

"But there will have to be reasons given when the case is heard."

"Next week," Mrs. Wiggin said.

"We sent you a letter about it."

"Did you receive that before you left?"

Harrison shook his head.

"We didn't know what else we could do."

"You say there is a hearing about this next week?" Harrison asked.

Both women nodded. "Thursday," Mrs. Wiggin said.

"That is in our letter too," Nevvie said.

"Oh boy," Harrison said.

"You will defend Johnny's claim, won't you, Harrison?"

"It was everything he had worked for."

Harrison puffed out his cheeks and then, slowly, exhaled through tightly pursed lips.

They were right, of course. That mine, whatever it was worth—and at the moment the value of the Amelia One seemed hardly of interest—really was everything John J. had worked for. To let it go to a bunch of strangers without protest would hardly be a fitting farewell to the best friend Harrison ever expected to have.

So now he was expected to show up in court within the week and prove a claim that was a total fabrication, made up by a pair of well-meaning women who had no idea of what he was supposed to prove, much less of how he was supposed to do it.

Great, he thought sourly. Just great.

CHAPTER 17

Harrison blinked, yawned and took another mouthful of oatmeal. It was good, but he would have preferred to have it after daybreak instead of before, thank you. Mrs. Wiggin had absolutely, positively insisted that he stay the night at their cafe the way John J.—although she had continued to call him Johnny—always had.

Harrison had given in as much because the woman would not take no for an answer as because he had no money to hire a proper hotel room.

A temporary bed had been made out for him in the public eating area, using a pallet and one of the long tables for his bed. The women, of course, had had privacy in the back portion of the tent.

According to Mrs. Wiggin, John J. had used the same arrangement for almost two months, since he began work on the development of the Amelia One. She said his intention had been to find a buyer for the house in Tonopah and then move permanently to Goldfield. But he had not had time enough to accomplish that before his death.

Harrison appreciated the women's hospitality. He truly did. But he would have also appreciated being able to sleep until a civilized time of morning. That was not possible with this arrangement.

Both Mrs. Wiggin and Nevvie had to be up and working by four, starting the fire in the big stove and getting bread and rolls into the oven. The table had to be cleared and Harrison's makeshift bed rolled up and put away before the cafe opened at 5:30.

Getting up at 5:25 would have been bad enough, but it was unavoidable that the noises of the women at work should wake Harrison long before that time. He had been awake, bleary-eyed and protesting but definitely awake, ever since Mrs. Wiggin and Nevvie had begun stirring.

64

Harrison finished his breakfast—at least he had been able to argue Mrs. Wiggin into accepting payment for any meals he took; he felt a little better after that—and began washing his utensils in the pail of hot water Mrs. Wiggin kept on the back of the stove for that purpose.

"Would you like this?"

Harrison jumped, startled. He had not heard the girl come up beside him. He thought both women were busy in the front room.

"What?"

She was holding out a leather case that Harrison did not recognize. "These were Johnny's. I thought you might like to use them. He left some of his things here. I . . . suppose they're yours now anyway."

"Thanks." Harrison accepted the small case and looked inside. It contained a pair of razors, soap, brush and hair brush.

"There's a strop around here somewhere," the girl said. "Johnny used to keep it hanging on the pole over there. We took it down after . . . you know."

Harrison nodded.

The girl rummaged in a box to find the strop while Harrison used the shaving brush and soap to lather his face. He let his whiskers soak while he stropped one of the razors.

"The mirror is over here," Nevvie said.

"Thanks."

"Would you mind if I watch?"

"What?"

"I asked . . ."

"I heard what you asked. It just surprised me. That's all."

She smiled. "Johnny used to let me watch him shave sometimes. The faces he made were just *aw*ful."

Harrison shrugged and went about the routine of shaving. He certainly was in need of it after the time he had spent on the road. He tried to remain oblivious to Nevvie, standing a few feet away and watching him intently while he contorted his jaw this way and that to avoid cutting himself with the feather edge of the straight razor. He could not help noticing, though, that her face alternately twisted and grinned as she unconsciously imitated his movements.

"Was that awful enough for you?" he asked when he was done and she handed him a towel to wipe the remnants of soap away.

"Ick! It was terrible."

He grinned at her. "Satisfied."

"Uh huh. Thanks."

"Anytime," he said. He glanced toward the roof of the tent, where morning sunshine was beginning to show a soft glow through the canvas. "Could you tell me how to get out to the Amelia One, Nevvie? I'd like to see what it's like."

"Of course."

She gave him directions, and Harrison got his coat and cap. There probably was no purpose in going to see the mine his friend had been developing, but Harrison wanted to see it anyway. It had been important to John J. and to these women.

A ten-minute walk took him to the site. The Amelia One was on the south slope of a low, barren knoll. There was hardly a leaf or a sprig of vegetation anywhere on the rocky soil. Or anywhere else in view for that matter.

But then men had not been drawn here by the prospect of raising crops on this ground. It was what the earth contained, not what it grew, that was of interest here.

Finding the Amelia One was difficult. There were claim markers covering the entire knoll, although no work appeared to be in progress on any of the claims as yet. The Amelia One showed the most development so far, and there was little enough of that.

John J. had begun a vertical shaft, presumably driving downward from the outcrop point where the ore body had first been discovered. Only large, well-financed companies could afford to locate an ore body in one place and then dig their shafts and tunnels for convenience instead of following the ore veins.

From the surface Harrison could not tell how far underground John J. had gotten before he died, but judging from the small size of the tailings pile behind the shaft opening, he had not gotten very far at all. A shaft of any great size or depth dislocates huge volumes of rock, and the trash pile beside the Amelia One's shaft was very small.

A thick plate of iron-strapped timbers had been laid across the shaft mouth, and there was a small scaffold above the opening where a hand-operated hoist was mounted. The plate, a trapdoor arrangement, was padlocked shut and a notice was tacked beside the lock proclaiming that the mine had been ordered closed pending settlement of the claim dispute.

John J. had also built a tiny shed, a wooden cube no more than five feet high, wide or long. Harrison assumed the shed had been put there to house hand tools like picks and drills, but it was empty now. Whether the court had also ordered it sealed he did not know, but now the door of the shed was hanging askew and the place was empty. Probably someone had come along and helped himself to the tools once John J. was not around to use them.

Harrison sat on a crossmember of the rickety hoist tower and remembered another, much larger and sturdier tower from long ago.

Long ago, he thought now. Not long after he had first met John J.

Harrison had been on the run then. From the courier guards he mistakenly believed were thieves and from John J. himself, who Harrison believed was trying to kill him for the stolen money in Harrison's possession.

That time Harrison had tried to hide under the hoist tower, not realizing what it was, and he had fallen into a mine shaft. It was John J. who had pulled him out, literally saved his life that night.

So long ago and so far away, Harrison thought now.

He wished he had been here to pull John J. out of trouble this time.

It might have been at this very place that John J. fell to his death. No one had ever said exactly how or where the accident had occurred, Harrison realized now. No one had told him. In fact, he could not remember who had told him that John J. died in a fall. Or they had told him and he had not been listening. That might well have been it. At any rate, he could not remember. It could have been right here.

And if John J.'s dear friend Harrison Wilke had been here, John J. might not be dead at this moment.

Harrison shuddered, thinking about that. That John J. had saved him in a similar situation once. But when John J. was the one who needed help, Harrison had been nowhere near to give it.

Harrison buried his face in his hands, and for the first time in a very long while he wept.

CHAPTER 18

They walked side by side, and although Nevvie was a small girl Harrison did not have to slow his pace to stay beside her. He had already noticed when she worked in the cafe that she was always busy, always quick. Not flighty in the least but very active.

He would have assumed that anyone maintaining that kind of working pace should have welcomed a rest in the afternoon—and in all probability she should be near exhaustion every night—yet now, in midafternoon when there was a lull in the activity in the cafe, she had volunteered to take Harrison to John J.'s gravesite on the edge of Goldfield. He had asked about the grave earlier, and she had quickly offered to go with him.

It was not far, no farther than the Amelia One, although in a different direction.

If Goldfield lasted long enough there would probably be a formal cemetery established here. So far there was only a deserted piece of dry, rocky ground where half a dozen headboards protruded from the earth. It was an unlovely place for a man to reach his end, Harrison thought.

"I hope someday people will put up a fence and make it . . . nicer," Nevvie said, as if echoing Harrison's thoughts.

"Someday," he murmured.

"It's this one over here," she said. She led the way around the other faded, warping boards to the last marker in the short row.

John J.'s name and the years of his birth and his death had been burned into the slab of wood at the head of his grave. The information was still legible, but it would not be for long. Already the effects of sun and drying wind were causing the slab to crack and turn brittle.

"Mama and I want to replace that with a real stone," Nevvie said, again uncannily joining her thoughts to Harri-

69

son's. "When we get the money to. We already asked Mr. Beck about it. He said we could have a granite stone cut and shipped in without it being too dear."

Harrison nodded. He, too, had thought about providing a stone, but it was just as well if Mrs. Wiggin wanted to do that for her Johnny.

Automatically he stood at the foot of the grave and removed his cap. But that was a matter of form and convention, not of feeling.

It surprised him, seeing John J.'s grave, but what he felt here was no more—perhaps even less—than he had felt at the mine or at the house.

This miserable, parched little piece of soil had nothing to do with the friend he had loved. John J. had never worked here, never laughed here, never loved here. The grave, it turned out, was only a place. The memories were all elsewhere.

While Harrison stood in silence, Nevvie was busy on her knees cleaning windblown litter away from the base of the marker. She tossed it aside, and Harrison could see that someone had embedded a glass jar in the ground at the foot of the slab. The jar held a forlorn assortment of dried weeds.

"Your mother?" Harrison asked, pointing to the arrangement.

Nevvie shook her head. "Mama can't bear to come here. She talks about coming. Most every Sunday she does. But she just can't bring herself to do it. She hasn't been back since the day Johnny was buried."

"Who then?"

Nevvie blushed.

"You?"

She nodded. "He was a good man, Harrison. He made my mama happy. She laughed when they were together. They both did. I wanted them to have that happiness for a long time. You could say that I loved him, too, though more as a friend than as a daughter."

"I think I can understand that," Harrison said. "What with your own dad being gone and everything."

Nevvie smiled, sadly he thought, and stood, brushing

the dust from her skirt where she had knelt. "Actually, Harrison, Johnny was as close to having a real father as I shall ever come."

"I don't understand."

"Johnny was everything Daddy was not. Cheerful and kind and loving. The kind of man who looked ahead. He wanted so much for Mama. And for you." She was not wearing a bonnet. A hot breeze came swirling past them across the desert to pluck at loose strands of her hair.

"I know I shouldn't speak ill of my own father," she said, "but he was Johnny's opposite in every way you can think of. Mama was better off when he left us."

"I thought you said he died."

She shrugged. "We heard that he did. It was probably so."

Harrison nodded. There was nothing uncommon about a man disappearing from one life into another. Harrison, John J., in a manner of speaking each of them had chosen to do so. But that choice was not so readily available to a woman with a child to rear.

"Johnny told about himself, of course. It was hard for us to believe that he could have spent all that time on the rods, the way he said he did. And you."

"He wasn't running away from anything," Harrison defended. "He was enjoying the freedom. John J. traveled from a love of the road, not for fear of anything that was behind him."

"And you, Harrison?"

He shrugged. "I buried my fears a long time ago." He smiled. "I think it's called growing up. It took me longer to do it than most, that's all."

"Johnny always told us that you are a better man than he."

"Johnny was a liar," Harrison said with a smile.

Nevvie gave him an odd, head-tilted examination that lasted long enough for him to begin to feel a trifle uncomfortable. Then she came to his side and took him by the elbow. "I think we should go back now," she said.

Harrison glanced down toward the grave. It was still only a place. It had nothing to do with the John J. he had known. "I think we should," he agreed.

CHAPTER 19

"Horst? Ralph Horst?" Harrison broke into a broad grin and held his hand out to the other man. "John J. wrote about you often, Ralph. He told me you were the best friend he had here. It's a pleasure to meet you finally."

Horst nodded. His expression, Harrison thought, was cordial but not exactly enthusiastic. "I heard a great deal about you, too, Mr. Wilke." They shook hands.

"But I thought you were over in Tonopah," Harrison said.

"I was," Horst explained, "but I moved over here when John did. We were both interested in the opportunities of the new find."

"Ralph helped Johnny with some of the development work on the Amelia One," Nevvie said. "Ralph helped him sink the shaft and get a start on the shoring. He rigged the hoist. All that sort of thing. Johnny said he didn't know what he would have done then without Ralph to help him."

"I'm glad you were here then," Harrison said, regretting that he had not been able to be there when John J. needed help but genuinely pleased that Horst had been able to offer it.

"Would you two excuse me, please?" Nevvie headed back toward the cafe, where her mother would need help now.

Harrison felt in his pockets, wondering if he had enough money left that he could afford to buy Horst a drink. He did. Tomorrow he could look for work to pay for his meals.

He made the offer, and Horst led the way to a small saloon that showed a belief in some degree of permanence for the camp. The place was built of mud-mortared stone and only roofed with canvas. Harrison bought two beers and helped himself to a plate from the free-lunch display.

"Are you still in the saloon business yourself?" he asked, trying to think back to the things John J. had written about his friend Ralph.

Horst shook his head. "I'm not a very good business-man. Proved that to myself in Tonopah." He smiled thinly. "I may well be the only human in captivity who can lose money tending bar in a mining town."

Harrison laughed and asked, "What are you doing now if you've given up mug-slinging?"

"Workin' for wages," Horst said. "I worked that bit for John. Then when he had his accident I found a job underground at the Shaky Lady."

"Shaky Lady? I don't think I'd want to work in a shaft that carried a name like that."

Horst shrugged. "The pay's good." The man seemed much more inclined toward seriousness than Harrison would have expected from the descriptions John J. had given. But then he and Harrison were strangers despite one mutual friendship. And there might well have been a touch of jealousy involved if John J. had praised Harrison to Horst as much as he had to Mrs. Wiggin and Nevvie. Close friendships could be like that, Harrison knew.

"Perhaps you could tell me something about the way John J. died?" Harrison asked. "No one really has, and . . . I'd like to know."

"Yeah, I can understand that." Horst took a deep swallow of the beer and set the mug firmly back down onto the table. "The way it was," he said, "John was on his way from here back to Tonopah. Don't know what for. He hadn't said anything to me about it that day. Anyhow, he was going back to Tonopah for something, to the house maybe, and his horse must of blown up on him. No one ever will know why, and I don't suppose it makes any difference anyway. The point is, the horse shied or what-ever, and John fell. Hit his head on a rock. Split his skull open, it did."

Harrison shuddered at the thought. Ralph Horst's expression when he said it was one of distaste. That, Harrison thought, was entirely understandable.

"I shoulda been with him," Horst said, "but like I said, he hadn't told me anything about going back there for any reason. We'd knocked off work about noon that day, and I went back to my place. I have a tent pitched not too awful far from the Amelia One. I figured he was going back to see Amelia. He was staying there, you know."

"Amelia?"

"Yeah. Miz Wiggin. That's her name."

"I thought the lawyer in Tonopah told me her name was Constance."

Horst shrugged. "Constance, that's her right and proper name for legal things, but everybody calls her Amelia. I think Amelia's her middle name, though rightfully she goes by Constance MacNeal Wiggin. Wiggin was her married name, of course. The other I'd guess was her daddy's name."

"So John J.'s new mine was named for her?"

"Sure. What did you think?"

"I guess . . . I don't know, that it was already named or something."

"Naw, John named it. For her. They was planning on getting married, you know."

"So I heard." Harrison took a sip of beer and popped a pickled egg into his mouth. The flavors went well together.

"Anyway, what I was saying," Horst rambled on, "John was on the road to Tonopah. Must have happened at night, because nobody noticed him laying there beside the road till the next morning. By then it was way the hell too late. From the looks of him, and I seen him afterward myself, it would have been too late even if somebody'd been right there beside him when it happened."

"You worked with him at the mine that morning, then that afternoon he was going to Tonopah?" Harrison asked.

Horst took a swallow of beer and nodded. "That's what I said."

"That doesn't make a lot of sense," Harrison said. "I was told the claim made by that California investment group was that John J. had lost the title to the mine to pay off gambling debts. I would assume he would have done his gambling in the evening. So how could he have been gambling and been on the way to Tonopah at the same time?''

''Never said it was the same time, did I?'' Horst asked. ''For that matter, I don't know nothing at all about that piece of paper they say John signed. But I see what you mean. He wouldn't have lost the Amelia One one night and then been out working her the next morning. An' I sure knew John well enough to know that he never got himself so drunk that he would forget a thing like that. Only way I can figure it, Wilke, is that he might of lost the paper—if he lost it—that afternoon or evening an' then been on his way to Tonopah afterward. Like I told you before, nobody seen it happen so nobody knows just when it was. Could of been that way, then, or could of been something else neither one of us will ever figure out. Fact is, John's dead. That's all the fact I really an' truly know about it all.'' He reached across the table and helped himself to a slice of ham off Harrison's plate.

''Could be,'' Harrison said. His thoughts, though, were no longer really on the conversation.

John J. had gambled. That was true. When he had a little money in his pockets, John J. thoroughly enjoyed a relaxing game of chance.

But he never bet heavily, at least not in Harrison's long experience with him, and he only rarely played cards. Generally he had preferred the excitement of dice or the roulette wheel to the quieter card games.

And it was inconceivable to Harrison that anyone, John J. in particular, would wager something as valuable as the title to a gold mine on something as nebulous as the roll of a pair of dice or the spin of a red and black wheel.

On the other hand, it had been three years since Harrison had spent any time in John J.'s company. In that time he had changed to the extent of becoming a settled, marriage-minded property owner with serious plans for the future. It was at least possible that he might have changed in other ways as well.

"Had John J. been gambling much before he died?" Harrison asked.

Horst shrugged. "Some. You know how it is. Generally speaking we'd finish work toward dark, then stop at the washstand behind the hotel to clean up on our way back. Maybe stop in here for a beer or over at the Golden Garter. It's a whole lot bigger place, and they have tables where a man can try and double his money. We'd have a beer or two, and John would play a spin or two on the wheel. Then we'd go over to Miz Wiggin's for dinner. After that we might smoke a pipe together, and I'd go back to my digs alone. I'm not sure if John went back out and played more or not. Could have been since he couldn't make out his bed an' get any sleep until the supper trade was clear over at Miz Wiggin's."

"He still liked the roulette then. And dice?"

"Yeah, sometimes."

"Cards?"

Horst paused for a moment. "Now that I think on it, he wasn't all that fond o' the pasteboards. Funny how I never noticed that before."

So that had not changed, Harrison thought. He found it interesting, if only because it was possible that a man might bet his whole bundle on a royal flush, say, or four aces. But not on the spin of a roulette wheel.

"He never mentioned anything to you then about this California group? An offer to buy the Amelia One or anything?"

Horst shook his head. "Never. Never heard of them people until Miz Wiggin mentioned them."

Harrison sighed and finished his beer. "Thanks for your time, Ralph."

"Yeah, sure," Horst said indifferently. He still seemed cool toward Harrison. "See you again, Wilke." The man rose and left the small saloon.

CHAPTER 20

Harrison finished scraping away the whiskers under his chin and wiped the razor free of soap on the towel. He looked into the mirror and found Nevvie looking back at him. She was behind his right shoulder. Slowly, his face still set in stern concentration, he crossed and then uncrossed his eyes. Nevvie burst into a peal of laughter, and he grinned.

The girl picked up another towel from on top of the butcher block and snapped it at him. The tip of it caught him in the small of the back and stung like fire.

Nevvie's eyes got wide. "I didn't mean to really . . ."

She was too late. Harrison already had his own towel in hand and was after her.

Nevvie ran shrieking into the front room with Harrison in close pursuit.

They dashed past Mrs. Wiggin, who was scrubbing the tables to prepare them for the breakfast crowd. She shook her head in mock disgust.

"Children!" she exclaimed. But she was smiling when she said it.

Besides, neither Harrison nor Nevvie was paying any particular attention to her at the moment.

Nevvie ran outside and around to the back of the tent, losing Harrison in the maze of support ropes that surrounded the canvas cafe. She was smaller, quicker and much more agile than he, and she was in much better condition.

Congratulating herself, she dropped to all fours, lifted the back wall of the tent and crawled inside.

She crawled into the kitchen only to find herself on hands and knees in front of a pair of heavy, masculine-styled shoes.

She looked up. Harrison was standing over her. He had

his towel drawn back and poised ready for a perfect, stinging snap.

"Oops," she said. And grinned. Harrison began to laugh so hard that he could not pop her with the damp end of the towel. She chimbed to her feet and ostentatiously wiped her hands on the towel she still held.

"You missed a place just to the right of your mustache," she said solemnly, as if there had been no interruption in his shaving.

Harrison felt of his cheek immediately to the right of his mustache. "I don't feel anything."

"Not there, silly. On the right."

"That is my right."

"Not from here it isn't."

He looked into the mirror. On the *left* side of his mustache there were a few stray hairs. "They can stay there until tomorrow, by golly. I'm breathing so hard now I don't think I could cut them off without taking half my face with them."

"Do you want me to do it for you?"

"You? What do you know about shaving a man?"

"Huh. I can do lots of things, mister smart aleck, that you don't suspect." She picked up the razor and flourished it in front of him, then turned the keen edge toward herself and blew on it.

"You can't be serious," he said.

"Of course I am." She took him by the arm and tugged him across the room to the stool and sat him down on it. "Now be still."

"I still don't think you can do it."

"Quiet," she ordered.

"Yes, ma'am."

Nevvie assumed a haughty, serious air that did not at all match her gay personality. She inspected him critically, tilting her head first one way and then the other, all the while wielding the razor under his nose.

"Would you be offended if I admit to nervousness here? Could we do this some other time, maybe?"

"Hush yourself."

Gingerly she touched the side of his nose with the

fingers of her left hand. "Humph." She tried it again, harder.

"Ouch."

"Don't be such a baby." She leaned closer. She had the tip of her tongue jammed into the corner of her mouth and protruding just a little. It looked comical, and Harrison had to work very hard at keeping a straight face.

It was not that he particularly wanted to keep a straight face. It was just that he was afraid she would end up slicing his nose off if he moved.

Nevvie leaned even closer and very gently applied the edge of the razor to his skin.

Her wrist turned a fraction of an inch, and he could feel the movement of the blade edge.

"There," she said.

"I'm impressed," he said.

He looked at her. Their eyes were no more than a few inches apart as she bent over him. So clear, he thought. And there were so many colors in those tiny flecks. Gray and green and gold and brown. He blinked and pulled away from her, his cheeks heating and a most unseemly stir of desire welling unexpected deep in his groin. He hoped desperately that she would not notice.

Nevvie turned away to find the towel and wipe the razor clean. Harrison felt a sense of intense relief, which served the added purpose of removing the cause for his embarrassment.

"Harrison?"

"Um?" She sounded serious now.

"I haven't ever seen you be . . . playful like that . . . before now."

"Really?" He shrugged. "I haven't been here very long."

"No, but, well, Johnny said that was the only thing he ever worried about where you were concerned. He liked you *so* much, and he respected you too. Did you know that? He really did. But he said you'd never learned how to play. He used to say that if there was just one thing he could give you, it would be for you to know how to play and just . . . have fun."

"I have fun," Harrison protested automatically.

Nevvie turned her head to look at him. She looked serious at first, but then she smiled. "So you do, Harrison. I'm glad."

He smiled back at her.

Of course he had fun, he told himself. Everyone has fun. He enjoyed a great many things. He just was not boisterous about it the way some people were. That was all. But sure he had fun.

He found it oddly disquieting, though, to think of John J. saying something like that after all the fun they had had together over the years.

He wondered if there might be something that he had not quite understood about it. But he did not want to discuss it right now.

Besides, he had to report for work in less than twenty minutes. If he missed the shift cage he would not have work for the day.

Nevvie threw him the towel so he could dry his face—although it felt somewhat too dry already—and he got his coat and cap.

Silly darn girl, he thought as he headed for the Dryden Three's cage hoist. But she did have awfully pretty eyes.

CHAPTER 21

"Mr. Frye?"

The lawyer looked up from the stack of paperwork on his desk. The desk, a chair and a single filing cabinet occupied very nearly the entire floor space of the tiny office. On the other hand, the office was contained within a building constructed of real bricks, not lumber or native materials, so the cost of building it must have been exorbitant so far from the railroad.

George Frye was middle-aged and already nearly bald. He looked neither more—nor less—seedier than most gold-camp barristers.

"I am he," Frye announced in a deep, precise voice. The voice alone, Harrison thought, would give the man a decided advantage in any appearances before a jury.

There was no lack of interest reflected in Frye's expression, although Harrison was wearing clothes that had been streaked with mud and coated with dust from several days of working underground. Today, though, Harrison had no time to earn a three-dollar wage. Mrs. Wiggin's—Harrison's—counterclaim against the Californians was to be heard in the morning, and Harrison still had no idea how he was expected to preserve John J.'s property.

For a moment Harrison was suspicious of a lawyer who would be so receptive to a hobo, which was how Harrison was beginning to regard himself again. Then he remembered that this was, after all, a mining camp. Here any bum could become a millionaire tomorrow. Or any millionaire could become a bum again in the same period of time. Harrison smiled and stepped forward to offer his hand.

He introduced himself. The name drew no response from Frye beyond a polite acknowledgment.

"I am here about the Amelia One," Harrison said.

Frye looked relieved. "The new representative, I take it?"

"I beg your pardon?"

"You are here to represent California Investments, Ltd., are you not, Mr. Wilke?"

California Investments, Ltd. That was the name Beechum had given him too, the investment group that now claimed ownership of the Amelia One. Harrison had not been able to remember for sure, although he had been close.

But why in the world would the group's own lawyer be asking Harrison if he were their representative. Odd, Harrison thought.

For a brief moment Harrison considered a pretense, letting Frye believe that he did represent the Californians in the matter.

Harrison smiled to himself. With his kind of luck, the lawyer's next words if he tried to do that would be a request for payment of fees. Better to straighten it out now, he decided.

"As a matter of fact," Harrison said, "I am not, uh, affiliated with CIL. In fact, sir, I am your opposition in the matter. I'm John J. Trohoe's heir and sole beneficiary."

Frye looked startled. "Really? I was hoping . . . Never mind." He sighed and looked down toward his papers for a moment.

When he looked up again he seemed sure of himself. "My sympathies, of course, Mr. Wilke, but I assure you the CIL claim of ownership of the Amelia One property is legitimate."

"I understand, sir, that that is what remains to be decided in court."

"A formality," Frye said with a wave of dismissal. "I have in my possession a certified copy of the transfer of title, signed by Mr. Trohoe shortly before his death."

"May I see it?"

"Of course." Frye turned his chair—the room was so small there was no need for him to rise—and pulled a brown folder from the middle drawer of his filing cabinet. He selected a sheet of paper—Harrison noted there were very few documents contained in the file—and handed it to Harrison.

The sheet was typed, double spaced, and required less than a page of space. It was a very simple statement headed "Bill of Sale," briefly describing the Amelia One claim by name and general description, and stating that John J. Trohoe, legal possessor of the claim, did herewith transfer all right and title to the aforementioned property to California Investments, Ltd., of Goldfield, Tonopah and Sacramento.

At the bottom of the typed wording there was a typed "/s/ John J. Trohoe" and below that a notary seal and statement of certification by the clerk of county court.

"Is this the document you intend to introduce as evidence tomorrow?" Harrison asked.

Frye smiled. "Hardly, sir. As I suspect you already know, a copy is not regarded as evidence when the original document is available. I intend to introduce the original as my evidence."

Harrison grunted. Too bad about that, he thought. At this point he was more than willing to settle for technicalities as his defense.

"May I have the names of your witnesses to the transfer, Mr. Frye?"

Frye smiled and spread his hands. "Mr. Wilke. I very much doubt that I shall need witnesses to a document that is quite able to stand on its own merits."

Harrison kept his face impassive, or hoped that he was successful at it anyway, but he felt a keen sense of disappointment. The only thing he had been able to think of so far was the hope that he might be able to discredit the man or men who claimed they had seen John J. sign over the mine.

So far, asking around in the watering holes of Goldfield and enlisting the reluctant help of Ralph Horst, he had not been able to locate anyone who said they had seen such a transfer. In fact, he had been able to find no one who admitted remembering having seen John J. in town at all that evening.

"Just who is this California Investments, Ltd., Mr.

Frye? No one I ask seems to know anything about them here.''

''The validity of the claim does not rest on that information, Mr. Wilke. Nor am I required to disclose it to you.''

Harrison smiled. ''What you are saying, sir, is that you would not have to tell me. If you knew.''

''What are you implying, Mr. Wilke?''

Harrison shook his head. ''Nothing, Mr. Frye. I'm just curious. That's all.''

Frye relaxed a little and smiled. ''To tell you the truth, sir, so am I. But my retainer was paid in advance, and the claim appears to be entirely valid.''

Harrison thanked the man and left the tiny office. The visit seemed to have been a complete waste of time, but the effort had had to be made.

He reached the street and glanced up at the sky. It was nearing noon, and he was beginning to get hungry. He turned toward Mrs. Wiggin's cafe and a lunch that probably would not sit well on a troubled stomach.

CHAPTER 22

They arrived well in advance of the scheduled 10 A.M. appearance time, Harrison and Mrs. Wiggin and Nevvie. Mrs. Wiggin had shooed her breakfast customers out by eight o'clock and hung a "Closed" sign on the front tent flap, and both women had put on their best.

It was the first time Harrison had seen either of them in anything but their working clothes. Mrs. Wiggin looked matronly and dignified in an aged but decent quality plum-colored dress. Nevvie looked young and, Harrison thought, a trifle awkward in an old-fashioned blue dress that looked like it had been cut down and altered to fit her. The girl did look rather pretty in spite of all that though, he thought. She had even stayed up late the night before with the stove and heating irons to curl her hair.

The day was fine, thank goodness, because there was neither a courthouse nor a courtroom in Goldfield yet. The session was held out of doors, with tables and benches arranged for the contesting parties and a larger table for the presiding judge. Spectators were expected to make their own accommodations for seating if they so desired.

The judge was a young man. Unconsciously Harrison had been expecting an elderly gentleman with white hair and perhaps snowy chin whiskers. Instead the judge was younger than Harrison, with a full beard and a freshly brushed suit of clothes. He wore a wide-brimmed hat against the glare of the sun and a large, gaudy ring that sparkled every time he raised his hand to stroke his beard, which he did frequently. He looked bored, as if he were scarcely paying any attention, with the testimony that was in progress when Harrison and the Wiggin women arrived.

They stood at the back of the assembled crowd—a considerable gathering of fifty or more people—and waited for their turn before the bench.

It was impossible to hear anything that was being said by the litigants already before the judge. The spectators, or possibly they were all appearants, talked while they waited, and there were no small number of flasks and pint bottles in evidence too.

Harrison was able to find an empty crate discarded behind the nearby claims recording office, which he converted to use as a stool for Mrs. Wiggin. He and Nevvie had to stand.

Attorney Frye was on the far side of the crowd talking with a group of working-class men who looked like they had been called away from their shifts to be there. Frye seemed at ease today. He was carrying a brown folder that Harrison thought he recognized.

The buzz of many conversations continued for a time, then there was a lull as the crowd's attention was drawn toward the front of the court area. A man in a business suit, who Harrison assumed must be the court bailiff, loudly called out a case and docket number and then the names, "Wiggin versus California Investments, Ltd. Contest of claim."

"That's us," Harrison said. He offered Mrs. Wiggin his arm and went with her to the recently vacated plaintiff's table. Nevvie trailed along with them. Frye made his way to the other table.

"Both parties are present, your honor," the bailiff announced. Behind him the crowd had begun to buzz again in their own private conversations, paying little if any attention to the proceedings at hand.

The judge, whose name Harrison never did get, rapped his table with a polished hardwood gavel. "Proceed, please. Mrs. Wiggin, I believe you are the complainant here."

She rose, glancing nervously over her shoulder as if to reassure herself that no one was really paying much attention. Harrison felt sorry for her.

"You are Constance Wiggin?" the judge asked.

"Yes, sir, rightly. But everyone calls me Amelia."

The judge nodded. He obviously did not care a fig what people called her. From this closer point of view Harrison could see that young as the judge was he was already tending toward a thickness around the middle. Harrison decided that he was probably thinking about lunch instead of this case.

"Well?" the judge prompted. "You filed this action. You must have something to say about it."

"Yes, sir, I . . ." She paused and stammered for a moment. "What it is, your honor, I filed that to stop those people from taking over what isn't rightfully theirs. The mine really belongs to Mr. Wilke here. He is Johnny, I mean Mr. Trohoe's, heir. Mr. Trohoe left everything, and that would mean the Amelia One, too, to Mr. Wilke. Those California people just don't have any right to it."

She stopped talking. After a moment of silence she sat abruptly.

A hint of a smile tickled the corner of the judge's mouth. "I take it that is the extent of your knowledge, Mrs. Wiggin?"

She nodded.

"Thank you." He looked at Harrison. "You are, um . . ."

Harrison stood. "Harrison Wilke, your honor. Of Denver, Colorado."

"And you have knowledge of this matter, sir?"

"Yes, sir, I do." He produced the papers Beechum had given him and took them forward to lay before the judge. The judge read them and returned them to Harrison.

"What do you have to refute the claim by"—he glanced down—"California Investments, Ltd., Mr. Wilke?"

"Just that, your honor."

Mrs. Wiggin stood and injected, "But Mr. Trohoe never signed over that mine, your honor. He would have told me if he had done a thing like that. We were going to marry, your honor. That mine was going to provide for us." She was speaking more strongly now, her initial fears ebbing if not totally forgotten. Behind her the crowd was a little less noisy, a bit more attentive.

"Thank you, ma'am, but that hardly constitutes proof." The judge looked toward Frye, who came forward now and opened his folder.

"If it please the court, your honor," he began.

The judge smiled. "What would actually please the court at this moment, sir, would be shade and an iced drink, but by all means continue."

Frye flourished a paper and presented it to the judge. "This is a holographic transfer of ownership, your honor, made out by one John J. Trohoe, conveying full right and title of the Amelia One property to California Investments, Ltd."

"I see." The judge looked it over. Then he looked at Harrison and raised an eyebrow.

"May I see the bill of sale, sir?"

"Of course."

Harrison took it. The wording was exactly the same as the certified copy he had seen in Frye's office, but this paper was handwritten and signed in the same hand.

"Your honor," Harrison said, "this document is meaningless. It was *not* written by John J. Trohoe, and that is not his signature either." He handed the paper back to the judge and glared at Frye, who seemed not at all disturbed by Harrison's claim.

CHAPTER 23

There was not exactly a dramatic stir as a result of Harrison's declaration. In fact, no one among the spectators seemed to have heard it. The judge looked at him and asked, "Do you have any proof of that, Mr. Wilke?"

"Of course, your honor. I've been receiving letters in John J.'s handwriting for years. There is no way I could possibly mistake it. This bill of sale was not written by John J. Trohoe. I will swear an oath on that, sir."

"You already are under oath," the judge reminded him.

"Yes, sir. But you know what I mean."

"Your honor," Frye said. "If it please the court?"

"Yes, George?"

"Need I point out, your honor, that Mr. Wilke is hardly a disinterested party in this matter? The man stands to gain ownership of a gold mine, of undetermined value, I grant you, but a gold mine nevertheless, if you accept his unsubstantiated claim here."

"You need not, George. I am well aware of the matters at stake here."

"Yes, your honor." Frye said it smugly rather than with contrition. His point had been fully made.

The judge turned back to Harrison. "Do you have any physical evidence to support your postion, sir?"

"I . . ." Harrison thought for a moment. Certainly he had none with him. The will Beechum gave him had been typewritten.

Back in Denver? He tried to remember what he might have done with John J.'s last letter. That had been some time ago. And unlike John J., Harrison had not saved all of his best friend's letters. He sighed and shook his head. "No, sir."

The judge spread his hands, as if in apology.

"Your honor?" It was Mrs. Wiggin. She was standing

again. Now she moved around from behind the plaintiff's table and came to stand beside Harrison in front of the judge.

"Did you have something to add, ma'am?"

"Yes, sir, I . . ." She dropped her eyes from the judge and began to blush. "I have . . . certain letters. They were sent to me by Mr. Trohoe when he was still living in Tonopah and coming over here occasionally. Sir."

"Are those letters signed?"

"Yes, sir."

"Your honor. If it please the court. I must most *stren*uously object to this . . ."

"Hush, George," the judge said patiently. "I am well aware of the objection you are about to introduce, but I remind you that Mrs. Wiggin has no apparent motive of gain if Mr. Wilke should prevail. I also remind you that Mrs. Wiggin has not had an opportunity to examine the document you have introduced into evidence here. Her offer is one of corroboration through physical evidence, but it remains to be seen which viewpoint would be corroborated."

Frye smiled. Obviously that thought had not yet occurred to him. Just as obviously, Harrison thought, if any scheme were afoot here to improperly gain control of the Amelia One, George Frye was not a knowing partner to it.

"Objection, George?"

"Not at all, your honor."

"Mrs. Wiggin, would you mind producing the letters you mentioned?"

She sighed. "No, sir. But I'd as soon you didn't let anybody else see them. If that would be possible, sir."

The judge spread his hands again. "Once they are introduced into evidence, ma,am . . ."

She flushed again. Then her jaw took on a set of determination. "I'll get them, your honor."

"Thank you."

She went off in the direction of the cafe. The judge turned back to Frye. "Have you anything beyond your physical evidence, counselor?"

"Yes, sir. Since this will take some time anyway, I may

as well introduce witnesses who will verify that John J. Trohoe was fond of gambling and that he was seen at the gaming tables on the evening before his untimely death.''

"Very well, Mr. Frye. Mr. Wilke, you are not an attorney and so I shall advise you, you have the right to listen closely to each of Mr. Frye's witnesses and at the conclusion of their testimony to question each of them on the subjects that have been raised during their direct testimony."

"Thank you, sir."

Frye motioned to the group of men he had been talking with earlier. One by one they were brought to the chair that had been placed near the judge's table, sworn to tell the truth and briefly questioned.

Each of them told approximately the same tale. Yes, John J. had been a frequent visitor to the gambling tables. Yes, they had seen him gambling the night before he died.

Harrison did not recognize any of the men. His own inexpert efforts to find witnesses had not led him to any of them.

But even he had to admit that they looked and sounded like honest men who had nothing to gain or to lose in this case. He did not believe any of them was lying.

Under his cross-examination, each of the men said that, no, they had not known how much John J. might have won or lost during a given evening of play. No, they had not actually seen him transfer title to the Amelia One to anyone on that or on any other evening.

"Mr. Frye," the judge said after the fourth man had testified.

"Yes, your honor?"

"You have the prerogative to call as many witnesses as your case requires, but I notice that this line of testimony appears to have found a rut to travel in. And that Mrs. Wiggin has returned."

"Yes, sir." Frye turned and motioned the rest of the men away.

Harrison noticed that Ralph Horst was among them. The man looked distressed. No doubt, Harrison thought, he was embarrassed because he had been called here to testify in opposition to a dead friend's interests. Harrison was glad Horst had not been required to take the stand.

Mrs. Wiggin came forward again and handed the judge two obviously much-handled, rather tattered envelopes. From where he stood Harrison could see that the envelopes had John J.'s name and Tonopah address for a return address and that they had been sent to Amelia Wiggin in Goldfield. The letters must have been sent fairly early in the courtship. And perhaps read repeatedly since John J.'s death. He hoped the court would see fit to return them to her when this case was concluded. Those letters were probably about all she had to remember him by.

The judge examined the outside of the envelopes first, then removed a flimsy and worn sheet of paper from one of them. Mrs. Wiggin turned away and began to blush furiously while the judge read.

Harrison thought the judge, too, colored. After a moment he coughed into his fist and hastily returned the letter to its envelope. "I, uh, believe I can use the handwriting sample on the, uh, envelope as an adequate example of Mr. Trohoe's handwriting, Mrs. Wiggin."

"Thank you, sir," she whispered.

"Objections, counselor?" the judge asked harshly.

Frye looked slightly startled. He had been about to say something, but he changed his mind. "Of course not, your honor."

"Good."

Harrison had no idea what was contained in the letter. He was glad that he did not. He only hoped now that the judge was as honorable a man as he appeared. Regardless, though, the delivery of those letters to another's hand must have been difficult for Mrs. Wiggin. He admired and grieved for her.

"May I have that bill of sale again, please?" the judge asked.

"It is still on the bench, your honor," Frye said. "There, I believe."

"Oh, yes. Thank you." The judge pulled the bill of sale in front of him, then one of Mrs. Wiggin's envelopes. He placed them side by side and bent over them.

"Well, your honor?"

The judge leaned back in his chair. "George," he said, "someone has been trying to make a monkey of you."

"Charlie!"

"Sorry, George, but these two documents were not written by the same hand. It's as plain as this damned, awful sunshine. Take a look for yourself."

Frye did. After only a few seconds his expression turned to disgust. "If I ever see that son of a bitch again . . ."

"Careful, George. You're under oath here, you know."

"Good. I meant it." Frye snatched up the spurious bill of sale and stalked away from the table.

The judge smacked the tabletop with his gavel. "Court rules for the plaintiff and the intercessor," he said. "The property known as the Amelia One to remain in the possession of Mr. Harrison Wilke of, uh . . ."

"Denver, sir."

"Thank you. Mr. Harrison Wilke of Denver, Colorado." He whacked the table again, and the bailiff picked up the docket sheet that would identify the parties to be called for the next case.

The judge handed Mrs. Wiggin her letters, and Harrison gave her his arm. She was trembling slightly when he led her back toward the cafe.

CHAPTER 24

Harrison had expected to feel excitement now. No, he decided after a moment, he had not honestly expected to feel excitement, he now believed that he should be excited. In truth, though, he had not really expected to win the case against Frye. Probably if the lawyer had been a dishonest sort who knew there was something wrong afoot, he could have won the case for his clients simply by paying witnesses to lie and claim they had seen John J. sign the bill of sale. He sighed. Regardless of all that, the fact was that he now owned the Amelia One. He supposed the proper thing to do next would be to open the shaft and try to determine how much, if any, potential the property had. After that he could decide what to do with it. In the meantime he felt . . . upset. This California Investments outfit had tried to swindle John J.'s memory.

Probably, Harrison thought, someone had come up with the plan as soon as it was learned that John J. was dead.

Why anyone would do a thing like that was clear enough. Greed was a more than ample motive for nearly anything as far as some people were concerned.

Who? Now that was another question entirely. Harrison was curious about it.

Not that it really mattered, though. John J. was dead. It was only his dying wishes that needed to be preserved now, and the court had taken care of that.

They reached the cafe, and Nevvie unpinned the "Closed" sign from the front flap.

"Hurry and change," Mrs. Wiggin told her daughter. "We have to get busy or they'll be clamoring for their lunch, and we won't have a thing to feed them."

Nevvie nodded and hurried toward the back of the cafe, but her mother lingered near the front with Harrison.

"I want to thank you," Harrison told her. "That was a brave thing you did, bringing out those letters."

The woman blushed again, and Harrison was once again grateful that he had not had to read whatever was in those letters.

"Will you be operating the Amelia One?" Mrs. Wiggin asked.

"I haven't thought that far ahead," he admitted.

She unpinned her hat and removed it. She held it in both hands, turning it around and around nervously.

"What is it, ma'am?"

She began to speak, stopped herself, then smiled. "Nothing, Harrison. Just my own emotional state, I'm sure."

He did not believe that, but he did not want to press her if she would find it, whatever *it* was, uncomfortable. "All right."

"Thank you." She reached up and touched the side of his cheek in a gesture that was almost motherly. Then she was gone, off to change her clothing and join Nevvie in frantic preparations for the lunch trade.

Harrison knew they did not need him underfoot at such a busy hour, and he was not really very hungry after the tensions of the morning. He checked his pockets. He still had several dollars left from the past few days of labor he had performed. A drink might help settle his nerves and his stomach, he decided.

"I'll be back later," he called toward the back of the cafe.

He drifted through the dusty, wheel-and-hoof-churned streets of Goldfield. He was becoming a little weary of tents and crude structures, so he went to the largest and finest of the town's saloons. It was, he remembered as he entered and saw the roulette wheel, the place where John J. had frequently liked to spend a few minutes at the tables in the evenings.

Harrison recognized several of the men there, including a number who had been called to testify for Frye this morning. He nodded to them pleasantly enough. They had all seemed honest, and he bore them no ill will. As far as he could tell they had simply been asked some questions and responded with the truth. He could hold that against no one.

He drank one beer, then ordered another and helped himself to a plate of the free lunch. He carried both to a table and sat.

"You," he heard a voice behind him. "Are you satisfied now, damn you?"

"What?" He turned. The man at the table behind him was John J.'s good friend Ralph Horst.

"I asked if you're satisfied now, damn you." The man was quite upset—and perhaps more than a shade on the drunk side as well—which Harrison thought was odd indeed.

Horst had been called this morning ready to testify. But then so had a good many others. Harrison found no fault with this.

Yet now obviously Ralph Horst was finding fault of some kind, and Harrison did not understand it. John J.'s wishes had been carried out. Surely that should have pleased any friend of his.

"I don't understand," Harrison said.

"Huh!" Horst snorted loudly. "Got your damn way now, don't you. Damn namby-pamby clerk, come in here with nothing and now you're the big man. Own your own mine, don't you, though you never felt the haft of a pick nor swung a singlebit nor packed a charge to earn the damn thing. No, not you. You just come in an' take over." The man belched and glared at Harison.

"I see," Harrison said calmly. "You think you should have the mine, do you?"

Horst's face flushed a quick red. "Me? *Me?* I'm not the one John wanted that mine left to, you stinkin' little bug. Not me an' not you.

"I thought I understood," Harrison said. "Obviously I do not."

"Huh!" Horst said again with an explosive snort of disbelief.

"I tell you, man, I have no idea what you are talking about. If you were as good a friend as you claim to have been, Ralph, perhaps you should tell me what it is you think John J. really wanted."

"Bastard." Horst mumbled.

"Are you going to tell me or not?"

"You already know. You just want excuses."

Harrison smiled at him. "Then you can deny me all excuses by telling me, can't you."

Horst sniffed and wiped his nose with the sleeve of his coat. "You expect me to believe he never told you, close as you two was?"

"Told me what, Ralph?"

"About him and the widow lady."

"You mean Mrs. Wiggin?"

"Who the hell else would I mean?"

Harrison shrugged. He explained to Horst why John J. had never written to him about the engagement.

"You serious?" Horst demanded.

"Of course."

Horst shook his head. "That's one of the things John told me," he said. "Not more'n a week before he died. We was talking about the wedding plans. An' the trip to Denver, that too. He was looking forward to it."

Harrison took a sip of his beer and waited for the tiddly man to go on.

"One of the reasons I couldn't shine to you any," he said.

Harrison had wondered about that too.

"What he told me. He was going to the lawyer next time he got over to Tonopah. Gonna change his will, he said. Gonna change it in favor of Miz Amelia Wiggin Trohoe. That's what he said he wanted done. Thinking of her name about to be Trohoe, he really got a kick out of that."

"I didn't know," Harrison said.

"About the change?"

"About the change or for that matter about the first will. He never wrote me any of that. Not a word."

"You serious, Wilke?"

Harrison nodded.

Horst sounded like he was telling the truth, Harrison thought.

And more than that, Harrison should have thought of this likelihood himself.

It was, after all, only logical and reasonable that a man should want to have his wife—in this instance his very soon wife-to-be—named in his will, particularly when there was property involved that could be valuable.

Harrison sighed. He felt like an ass. He should have realized, he told himself. But he had not.

Damn.

He turned his back on Horst, forgetting the man completely in the rush of Harrison's own thoughts, and ate his lunch without tasting a bite of it.

By the time he finished he knew what he intended to do.

CHAPTER 25

Harrison approached Nevvie first. By now he was coming to know Mrs. Wiggin well enough to realize that the woman had a great deal of pride . . . but an even greater regard for John J. and his memory. Harrison was afraid that, everything being as it was, Mrs. Wiggin might feel compelled to lie to him out of pride and of respect for John J.'s wishes.

He found the girl in the front portion of the cafe scrubbing the tables. The lunch trade had cleared out. Mrs. Wiggin—he checked—was in the back beginning preparations for the evening meal.

"Need some help?" he asked.

Nevvie lowered her eyes. He thought her cheeks colored slightly as well. "You don't have to do that."

"I don't mind," he said. He took the scrub brush from her, dipped it into the bucket of hot, soapy water she had set at the end of the table and began to briskly scrub away the stains and the crumbs left behind by the lunch customers.

The girl worked beside him, using the edge of her hand to wipe the standing water from the places he had just scrubbed and then drying the tabletop, more or less, with a towel. The earth floor suffered by that treatment, a thin line of dark mud forming beneath the tabletop edges like a poorly drawn outline, but the proper result was obtained above.

With Harrison's help the work went quickly.

During the past week Harrison had become increasingly comfortable as a more-or-less part of the Wiggin household. He liked Mrs. Wiggin, and he enjoyed talking with Nevvie. The girl was at times a chatterbox, rambling easily to her mother or to Harrison or to whoever else was near. Now, though, she was quiet as they worked together. The pleasure and the excitement of the morning at court seemed to have been pushed aside by some other thoughts or considerations.

"Could I ask you something?" Harrison ventured when they were on the second table.

"Of course." She said that as if it could not be in doubt, but she still did not look at him. Her attention was on the table surface. She used her thumbnail to chip at a dollop of dried grease that Harrison had missed.

"It's about John J. and your mama," Harrison said.

She looked at him now. He was not sure, but he thought she seemed angry. Or close to anger. "That letter was . . ."

"It isn't about the letter," he said quickly. "I don't care what was in the letter. That's private."

"What then?" Her eyes dropped away from his again, and she began to wring out her towel. Her nails, he saw, had been abraded short by hard work and were chipped at the tips. For the first time in almost a week he was reminded of Martha Blakemon, of the contrasts between her position and her grooming and this slight, busy child of the mining camps.

"John J. and your mama planned to marry," he said. He paused.

Nevvie shrugged. "They deserved the happiness. It just wasn't to be."

"I wish they'd had that time, too, but they didn't." Harrison paused again and scraped the bristles of the brush feebly over the wooden surface of the table. "It occurs to me, though, that John J. and I were friends. Good friends, of course. But we didn't have the special closeness that a man and wife are supposed to have."

Nevvie's chin shot up and her eyes grew wide. "Harrison! Surely you don't think that I . . . that anyone . . . you aren't trying to tell me, are you, that you think *I* thought that you and Johnny were . . . odd?"

It took a moment for Harrison to realize what she meant. Then he laughed. He threw back his head and laughed.

He sat on the bench in front of the table they were washing, took her hand and pulled her down beside him, still laughing.

"Good Lord, Nevvie. No, I never meant that." He

caught his breath and borrowed her towel to dab at his eyes. "No," he said, "that never would have occurred to me. Or to John J., I'm sure." He chuckled again. "Hardly."

He sighed. "I'm not making my point very well here, am I?"

"I don't think you are, Harrison."

"Okay. Let me try again. What I'm trying to get at is this: John J. and I were really good friends. But he *loved* your mama. He wanted to take care of her and protect her and provide for her for the rest of their days. Right?"

She nodded, obviously still far from understanding what he was trying to say or to ask.

"Right," Harrison repeated himself. "And if they'd gotten married, everything John J. owned would have been hers. That's the right and the proper way of things. It would all have become hers when he died."

"So?"

"So I'm betting that John J. never *really* meant to leave me everything in his will. He just hadn't had time to get the thing changed around. I mean, here he was working in Goldfield at the mine he named after your mama and staying with you folks the way I've been doing, and the house and lawyer and will and everything were over in Tonopah, and he just never had or took the time to do anything about that, seeing as how he never realized that he was going to die so soon like he did." He ran out of breath and stopped to look at her. "Am I right?"

She shrugged.

"They'd talked about it, hadn't they?"

Nevvie shrugged again.

"Please. This isn't a matter of being disrespectful to John J. or his wishes. Just the opposite. And I'd really like to know. Uh, Ralph Horst said John J. had told him he intended to make that change. I should have thought of it myself, but I didn't. It makes sense, though."

She shrugged again. "They talked about it. I was there when they did once. Johnny was telling Mama about the things he wanted to leave you when he changed the will. He was telling her if she had any objections he'd like to know them before he wrote any of it down. That he knew you wouldn't care if there was some things she wanted to save as keepsakes. Then he laughed, real short and low like he used to do when he was remembering something, and he said how you wouldn't care now but you sure would have back when he first met you. He said you'd come awful close to being a stuffy little prig then, but he'd saved you from all that. Then he laughed again.''

Harrison chuckled now. "He was telling the truth, you know. Lordy, do I owe that man.''

"Anyway,'' Nevvie said, "they talked about it that night. I think that was . . . oh . . . two weeks or more before the accident. So I guess he had time to change the paper but he just never got it done in time.''

Harrison smiled and squeezed the girl's hand. "Thank you, Nevvie.''

"Why?''

"Because I think we're all more interested in what John J. really *wanted* than in what any piece of paper says.''

"I don't understand.''

He grinned at her. "You will. And I'm going to need your help if your mama balks when I bring Lawyer Frye here this afternoon.''

"I still don't know what you mean, Harrison.''

"I mean I think that George Frye is a decent, honest enough sort. And we aren't on opposite sides of anything anymore. So I'd like him to draw up the paper and witness it when I deed the Amelia One back to your mother, as John J. truly wanted it to be done.''

"But Harrison . . .''

He jumped up, pleased and excited now, talking while he thought. "And I even know just who I want to get for one of the witnesses too. I want Ralph Horst to be here and sign that deed as a witness, by gum.'' He laughed.

"Surely you can't . . .''

"But Nevvie, surely I *must*. Can you seriously think I only cared about my best friend when he was alive?''

She shook her head.

"Good. So help me when your mother tries to tell me we can't do what John J. wanted us to do. You go fuss at her," he said. "I'll go get Lawyer Frye and find the witnesses. We'll be back soon."

He grabbed up his cap and pulled it on, then dashed out of the tent in search of George Frye and Ralph Horst and whoever else was handy to serve as a witness.

Harrison felt better about this than he had felt about anything since he heard the news of John J.'s death. It felt *right*. And he was pleased.

CHAPTER 26

They stayed up later than usual that night, celebrating John J.'s memory with baked brisket and a cherry cobbler after the supper crowd was gone and the dishes washed.

Mrs. Wiggin had objected to Harrison's plan, as he had expected, but the argument that her Johnny's wishes should not be denied finally brought her around. Nevvie and, unexpectedly, George Frye had been a big help there. And Horst. Ralph Horst had told her in considerable detail how John J. had intended to have his will changed weeks before he died.

Harrison was grateful to all of them. Now that the Amelia One belonged to Amelia Wiggin he still felt that he had done the right thing, that he had done what John J. would have wanted him to do. And what John J. would have done for him if the circumstances had been different. Harrison could not ask for better than that.

He stuffed himself with the meal Mrs. Wiggin had prepared just for the three of them and almost wished he enjoyed smoking so that he could take a cigar after the meal . . . if he had a cigar. He laughed at himself and felt of his pockets. After paying George Frye's fee he doubted that he had enough cash left to buy himself a cigar if he *did* enjoy them. Perfect fiscal timing for the giving away of stray gold mines, he thought with a quiet smile.

But then that was one of the many things John J. had taught him through all the years. That it was what a man was and not what he had that truly mattered, that what he did with himself was more important than what he did with his possessions.

So yes, Harrison thought now, he still felt entirely pleased with the course of this day, from the victory in court to the transfer of the Amelia One to Amelia Wiggin. Harrison could scarcely remember a finer day.

He covered his mouth to conceal a contented belch, and Nevvie apparently mistook the gesture for a stifled yawn.

"You must be getting tired," she said. "I'll help you make up your bed."

"Thank you."

Harrison fetched the wadded roll of bedding from the corner of the tent and carried it out to the nearly dark front area. The girl took the things from him one by one and laid them out on the table. She plumped the thin pillow that once had been John J.'s and laid it in place for him.

"There," she said, smoothing out a last, invisible wrinkle. "May I ask you something, Harrison?"

"Certainly."

"Will you have to go back to Denver now?"

"I hadn't really thought about that," he answered honestly. "I suppose so.

"Mama will need someone to operate the Amelia One for her, you know. You could do that instead."

Harrison chuckled. "There are a lot of things in this world that I don't know about, Nevvie. Mining for gold has to be right up there near the head of the list. Your mama needs someone in that mine who knows what he's doing. Besides, after all this trouble, girl, we still don't know if the mine has any value whatsoever. None of us has ever been down into it. It could be no more valuable than a hole in the ground. And too deep for a posthole at that. No, miss, I don't believe I would be doing you or your mother any favors by hanging on here and trying to take a living out of your mine.

"It was just a thought," she said.

"It was a generous thought too."

"This past week," she said, "I had almost forgotten . . . I know it isn't right of me, but the way you dress and the way you're so nice and everything, just like Johnny always said you were . . . well, I had kind of forgotten what an important man you are back in Denver, going to be an officer in the bank and everything."

Harrison laughed. "Important? Don't you know that John J. must've had some Irish in his blood? He had the gift of making things sound better than they really are.

Which is a polite way of saying it. No, girl, I'm just a hired man who has to dress decent when he goes to work."

"But Johnny told us they were going to make you an officer soon. And how you go to the balls and the galas in Denver. And they have electric lights there and ice-cream parlors and gasoline automobiles and . . . everything."

"There is all of that," Harrison admitted.

"It must be wonderful," Nevvie whispered. She sat on one of the benches.

Harrison sat beside her and patted her clasped hands. "Wonderful," he said, "is found in people, not in places. You and your mother are wonderful folks. That's more important than all the electric lights and automobiles in Denver. Believe me."

"Johnny used to say things like that."

Harrison laughed. "Where do you think I learned it?" He patted her hand again and stood.

Nevvie stood hastily, smoothing at her apron and at the long skirt of her drab work dress. She was just a wisp of a thing standing next to him in the near darkness. The top of her head barely reached his chin.

She seemed vulnerable. Yearning? She had never known the lights and the excitements and the entertainments of a major city. Harrison could remember how he used to yearn for them.

His hands began to rise toward her shoulders. And he thought her slim, white-aproned figure swayed a fraction of an inch closer to him.

Harrison's hands dropped back to his sides. He turned his head and feigned a cough.

"I should go now," Nevvie said.

He nodded. He could feel a curious sensation, almost like a fluttering emptiness, very deep in his belly.

"Good night, Harrison."

"Good night, Nevvie."

She turned and went quickly to the slit in the canvas drape that separated the tent into rooms.

She disappeared through it without looking back, unaware that Harrison stood rooted, watching her go.

Oddly, he found himself hoping that he did not snore when he slept. Although if he did both Mrs. Wiggin and her daughter would certainly be aware of that fact by now.

He sat on the bench and began to remove his shoes. He found that this time he was not looking forward to riding the rods home to Denver. If he had had the money he would have gladly paid for train passage, just to get the journey over with quickly.

CHAPTER 27

A thump. Or a thud. Then a crash. Very loud. Very heavy. It sounded like wood on wood.

Harrison came awake and sat upright with the rough woolen blanket dropping away from his chest.

He heard a deep voice cursing vulgarly and then an equally deep guffaw.

"Whyn't you trip an' fall down, you dumb bastard," a voice said.

The first voice suggested an impossibility. The second man laughed again.

Harrison blinked. He felt disoriented.

By the time he realized there were two men, two intruders, inside the tent, the men had already reached the dividing wall and passed through it. Back to where Mrs. Wiggin and Nevvie were sleeping.

One of the men must have walked into a bench and tipped it over against the legs of a table. That must have been the sound that wakened him.

But what were they doing here?

Harrison felt a chill surge up and down his spine. Mrs. Wiggin. Nevvie Wiggin.

Could there be any other explanation for the intrusion?

He flung the blanket aside and dropped off the table, not bothering to search in the darkness for his shoes.

It was almost but not quite fully dark within the canvas walls of the tent.

A little light came through the fabric, from distant lanterns, from the moon, he did not know.

He turned toward the "door" cut into the divider and was caught up short by the table he had just been sleeping on.

The men must not have known he was here, he thought.

It was too dark for them to see him. They thought the women were unprotected.

Harrison felt the chill race through him again. The women *were* unprotected.

That was one of the things John J. had never been able to successfully teach him. Harrison simply had not had John J.'s strength and coordination. He had never been able to learn the manly art of pugilism.

He had never particularly cared until now.

He groped around the table toward the back wall again.

He heard a gasp and a sputtering sound from beyond the canvas. It sounded like Mrs. Wiggin, he thought. He groaned softly to himself as he thought what her terror must be at this moment.

"Quiet," a voice ordered.

"We ain't gonna hurt you."

"Maybe."

Both men were talking. That was obvious. But their voices were so similar that Harrison could scarcely detect any difference between them.

He blundered over a bench and fell sprawling onto the earth floor.

"Take your hands away, dammit, an' calm down so's I can take my hand off'n your mouth," a voice said.

There was the faint creak of wooden cot legs shifting, then silence.

"That's better."

"We already tol' you, we ain't here to hurt you. Not that way. You don't gotta be scared o' that."

"We got something you want to sign."

"You do that, an' we go away."

"It's a lease."

"Fella wants you to sign him a lease on some property."

"You sign it. We go away. No problem."

"Hold still now."

There was a moment of silence and then the scratch of a match head and a quick flare of light. The light steadied and intensified. A moment later there was the sound of a glass chimney being returned to a lamp.

"There," one of the voices said with satisfaction.

"We brought a pencil for you."

"No, dammit, you don't gotta see what the rest of it says. Jus' sign where it shows there."

"What . . . ?" This newest voice was thin and frightened. Nevvie.

Harrison reached up, found the edge of a table and pulled himself erect. He felt a little dizzy and wondered if he had bumped his head when he fell. If so, he had not been aware of it at the time.

He took a step forward and lurched to the side, almost losing his balance. He felt woozy and wanted to throw up.

"I don't underst . . ."

"Dammnit, woman, we aren't here to take no shit."

"Sign it!"

"Mama?"

There was a flurry of movement behind the wall. Sounds of feet and hard breathing and then the loud, loud sound of flesh striking softer flesh.

Nevvie shrieked. Started to. It came out as little more than a squeak, then was cut short by the clamp of a hand over her mouth.

"Leave my daughter alone . . ."

Harrison flung himself forward, through the slit in the drape, into the bright light of the back room.

He could see one man clearly, kneeling at the side of Mrs. Wiggin's bed.

The other was behind Nevvie. The man had one arm clamped around her waist. His other hand was covering her mouth. She was struggling with the son of a bitch.

Harrison launched himself at the man who was holding on to Nevvie.

He threw a punch, the very hardest he had ever thrown in his life he was sure, to the right of the small of the man's back, just over his kidney.

The man grunted and turned pale.

He let go of Nevvie and turned, lashing out with a backhanded slash of his fist that caught Harrison on the forehead.

Harrison chopped at the man's throat. Missed. Took a low, vicious jolt in the belly.

He bent over, gasping for breath, and saw the man's knee rising toward his face.

The first blows had hurt. Harrison did not hurt anymore. He felt detached and quite calmly aloof from the whole thing.

He knew that he was lying on the floor, although he was not quite sure how he had gotten there.

There was some screaming going on above and around him.

Nevvie was yelling something about rape, although Harrison thought that an error.

There was some high-pitched yelling and some deeper-toned yelling and then from out beyond the canvas walls there was some more shouting going on.

Something, a boot he thought, thumped into the pit of Harrison's stomach and then another into his ribs. He could hear the impacts more than feel them. He felt a ringing numbness much like the sensation of being thoroughly drunk except that he was more lucid about it yet still had the numbness.

Nevvie was still shouting, "Rape! Rape!"

Outside there was quite a lot of noise and activity now.

Harrison smiled. That was one of the things you could count on in the roughest of camps. *No* one accepted any molestation of decent womankind.

One of the men barked something at the other.

There was an angry, beehive sound from the front of the tent. The decent menfolk of Goldfield had arrived.

The intruders dropped to all fours and scuttled beneath the back wall of the cafe into the night.

Harrison rolled his head so he could see upward. Nevvie was there. She seemed to be quite all right. She was wearing a flannel nightdress.

He found it much more comfortable to let his head sag back down. He could see then that her feet were bare. Her toenails were trimmed short. They were very clean.

Someone—a good many someones—were standing over him now.

He could feel himself being lifted to his feet.

111

The unwanted movement sent a spear of pain lancing through his ribs, and he felt faint.

"No!" Nevvie screamed as someone began to beat him.

Harrison's last thought was of embarrassment. He had come back into the women's private part of the tent wearing nothing but his underthings.

He found it quite a relief to be able to pass out then.

CHAPTER 28

Harrison groaned. He felt something cool and moist pass across his forehead, down to his cheeks and then against his lips.

He opened his eyes and found himself looking into the bright green-gold-and-hazel of Nevvie's eyes very close above his.

She smiled when she saw he was awake. She sat up, and he could see that she had a damp washcloth in her hand.

"Hi," she said. She tried to make it a cheerful greeting, but her voice had a brittle quality to it and her eyes were unnaturally bright with a sheen of unshed tears. "I'm glad to see you're awake. We were starting to get worried about you."

Harrison smiled back at her. "I'm just fine."

He tried to sit up but gasped and dropped back against the bed. The pain caused by his attempt to move was excruciating.

Nevvie looked worried. She leaned closer again, turned her head aside and called, "Mama. Mama?"

Mrs. Wiggin hurried to Harrison's side. She sat on the edge of the cot—he was aware finally of the fact that he was not in the restaurant portion of the tent on one of the tables as he had expected but instead was on one of the beds in the back room—and took his hand. "Lie still, Harrison."

"What happened?" he asked.

"There were two men . . ."

"I remember that," he said. "I mean later. Why am I here?"

Mrs. Wiggin frowned. Nevvie looked embarrassed.

"When our neighbors came in," Mrs. Wiggin said, "they thought you were, uh . . ."

"Oh."

"Nevvie was screaming and fighting with them." Mrs. Wiggin chuckled. "She kicked two or three of them and bit another, trying to protect you."

"They were awful," Nevvie said.

"They did just right," Harrison told her. "They were protecting you and your mama. I'm glad they did."

"By the time we straightened things out," Mrs. Wiggin said, "the real thugs had made their getaway. I recognized both of them. They won't be seen around here again, I promise you."

Harrison tried to inch farther up against the pillow that had been placed under his neck. Nevvie saw the tension and the aborted motion as pain stopped him. She gently lifted his head and repositioned the pillow for him.

"Thanks," Harrison said. He was having difficulty breathing, but from this new angle he could see why. Someone had taped his ribs, quite severely, with wraps of wide sheeting cloth. He motioned toward it with a hand—even his arms hurt from the vicious pummeling—and raised an eyebrow. When he did that he could feel a resistance to the movement of the skin on his forehead.

"Mr. Howe, he's one of the neighbors, wrapped your chest. We don't have a regular doctor in town, but I think that is what you are supposed to do. Mr. Howe said for sure some of your ribs are broken. And we put plaster on you everywhere we thought we should. The worst split was on your forehead. There's another place over your temple. And some scrapes here and there. We put some smelly goop on them. Something Mr. Howe gave us."

A sheet covered him to the waist. The tight wrappings covered much of his torso above the sheet. Harrison uncomfortably remembered his state of near undress earlier. He slid his left hand under the sheet to check and was vastly relieved to discover that at least he still had on his drawers.

Nevvie noticed what he had done and laughed. "You're decent, silly."

Harrison blushed a bright, startled red.

"Could we get you anything, Harrison? Are you hungry? Thirsty?"

His first thought was refusal. He had already caused them trouble enough. But he was thirsty, he realized. He had not noticed it before, but he was. The thought of food held no interest at all, however.

"A drink would be nice," he said.

"I'll have to ask Nevvie to run next door and see if Mr. Howe keeps something in his living quarters."

"I didn't mean that, ma'am. Water would be fine."

"Oh." She smiled. Nevvie went to get a cup of water from the barrel. There was no community water system in Goldfield as yet. Mrs. Wiggin had to pay to have the barrel replenished twice each day for use in the cafe.

It took both women to raise him enough that he could drink from the cup Nevvie brought, and even then it was done only at a considerable expense in pain on his part and effort on theirs. Harrison tried not to show any of the pain he was feeling. He began to think that perhaps he should not have rejected Mrs. Wiggin's offer of something stronger.

"I better let you get some sleep now," he said. "You have to get up so early."

Mrs. Wiggin and Nevvie looked at each other, and the girl laughed.

"What?"

She pointed toward the canvas roof, and Harrison realized for the first time that there was strong sunshine beating down on it and flooding through to fill the interior of the tent.

"What time is it?"

"Ten o'clock. Something like that."

"But . . ."

"It's all right, Harrison. If you're feeling better later we can open for the evening folks."

"But I don't want you to . . ."

"Hush." Mrs. Wiggin pressed his head back against the pillow, and Nevvie bathed his face again with the cool, wet relief of the washcloth. It felt good.

Harrison closed his eyes and let himself begin to drift away from them.

115

He regretted what they were doing for him, because it meant they would lose that much of their meager income. But at the moment he did not regret it so much that he was going to stay awake and worry about it.

CHAPTER 29

Nevvie spooned broth into his mouth with one hand and used the other to wipe his lips with a napkin. Harrison frankly did not believe he needed such attentiveness after a day and a half of recuperation. But she insisted, and he was not arguing with her. The truth was that he was enjoying it.

There were, however, other matters that he was more than willing to argue. Except Nevvie and her mother were not.

"I still think . . ."

She stopped his comment with another spoonful of the broth, slipping the spoon in when he opened his mouth to speak. "Hush," she said.

She leaned back and tilted her head to the side, inspecting him with a critical eye. "You know, Harrison," she mused, "I think you should quit shaving. I think you would look *so* distinguished with a beard. The very model of what a banker should be."

"Will you *please* listen to me," he pleaded.

"We already have," she said primly. She reached forward with the spoon again.

"I've had enough, thank you. And you haven't listened to me. You know you haven't. Not you and not your mama, either one."

"Of course we have." She wiped his mouth again.

This time he felt annoyed . . . and frustrated . . . by the attention.

"Nevvie. Please. You have to understand that those men will be back."

"They wouldn't dare show their faces in Goldfield again. The gentlemen here would grab them first thing, and they know it."

"That's what I mean about you not listening, dammit,"

he said, not even regretting the use of the vulgarity at the moment.

Nevvie looked surprised if not shocked. She had almost certainly heard much rougher language than that. But never from Harrison.

"I don't mean that those *particular* men will be back. But whoever sent them can hire others just like them. Surely you can't think that they came here on their own. Your own mother said they weren't a very bright pair. They wouldn't have thought of a lease as a way of getting control of the Amelia One."

"I don't believe anyone ever mentioned the Amelia One that night," she said.

"No one had to. Good grief, Nevvie, what else do you have that anyone would want to lease. The cafe? They were perfectly obviously wanting control of that mine. Which means that it must be valuable to someone. To you and your mother, I should think. Unless someone else comes in and finds a way to strong-arm it away from you."

"We have told you over and over, Harrison. No one can do that. Our neighbors are too close. Just like the other night. All we have to do is shout, either of us, and they will be here."

"Nevvie! Someone could murder you. Both of you. And come up with another scheme like they did with John J., present another false transfer of title. And then where would you be? Your neighbors couldn't do anything about that. Someone could come in and murder the both of you and be gone before any of the neighbors could get awake."

"Pooh, Harrison. If the Amelia One had been all that valuable, Johnny would have told us about it. He wouldn't have had to tell us. We would have seen it on his face the next time he came through the door."

Harrison sighed. This was exactly the same kind of pigheaded argument he had been getting from both of them all along. Neither of these women could believe that anyone would seriously want to hurt them for the unknown quantity of the Amelia One. Yet Harrison could think of absolutely no other reason for that nocturnal intrusion.

"Could we at least find out if the mine is so valuable?"

Harrison asked plaintively. "Could we at least do that much? I mean, no one we know has even been down into the thing."

"That isn't actually so, Harrison," Nevvie said.

"What do you mean?"

"Mr. Horst knows the Amelia One almost as well as Johnny did. After all, he helped Johnny open the shaft. He would certainly know. And he hasn't said a word about it."

"Do you think you could find him?"

"Oh my, yes. Mr. Horst has been taking most of his meals here again. He should be here in a few more hours."

"Really? I don't remember seeing him in here before."

"He used to eat here nearly all the time. You know. Before. Then he stopped coming for a while. Now he's back."

Of course, Harrison thought. When Harrison had arrived on the scene with John J.'s will in his pocket, Horst had been upset because his friend's wishes were being denied. Now that that had been straightened out, the man was coming back again. So that made sense.

"Could I talk to him when he comes again?"

"I'll ask him," Nevvie promised.

The interview that evering, however, turned out to be less productive than Harrison had hoped.

"No," Horst said, "that hole isn't what you would call a good find. Color, of course. John wouldn't have stayed with it if it hadn't shown some color. But he was hoping it would open up and get better as we went deeper. Never did that I saw. Twenty-three, twenty-four dollars to the ton or thereabouts. That sounds like a lot, but it's marginal for a small outfit. Takes a lot of work to haul a ton of ore out of a shaft, and then you still have to pay processing fees if you don't have your own stamp mill. The return is pretty short. Best thing in a situation like that, I'd guess, would be to hang onto it until some of the big companies are pinched for ore to process out of their own mines an' then sell it to them. The ladies wouldn't get rich off it anyhow, but that way they'd come out with a little cash in their pocketbooks. Or they could lease it out now to somebody and take their return on a royalty basis. No way to tell which would be better for them in the long run.''

"You never saw anything that looked like an outstanding vein, though?" Harrison asked.

Horst shook his head. "Nope. Never did.''

"What about the claims around the Amelia One?" he asked. "I noticed that everything around it has been filed on, but there doesn't seem to be any activity on any of those claims.''

"Same deal, I'd guess,'' Horst said, "or even worse. I remember they was all filed on and some exploration work done, but nothing ever came of it. What little there is on the Amelia One claim seems to be a single outcrop vein. And that one too poor to get excited over.''

Harrison sighed. This sort of information was hardy going to help him convince Mrs. Wiggin and Nevvie that there was still danger for them in their ownership of the Amelia One.

"Thank you, Ralph.''

Horst shrugged. "Anytime.'' He stood and turned toward the "door" to the front part of the cafe. "Anything I can get you, Wilke?''

Harrison shook his head. Then changed his mind. "As a matter of fact there is one thing you could do.''

"Yeah?''

"It's kind of embarrassing to ask one of the ladies to help me out back. Would you mind doing that before you go back to your meal?''

Horst did not look exactly pleased with the request, but he complied with it. Harrison was truly grateful. It was a genuine relief not to have to ask Nevvie or Mrs. Wiggin to give that assistance for a change.

CHAPTER 30

"I think I know what I'd like for you to do," Harrison told Mrs. Wiggin. "If you trust me, that is."

"We trust you, Harrison," she said. "Even if we did not know how completely Johnny loved and trusted you, we have come to know you well enough ourselves that we have no doubts about you. But is this another of your scare things, trying to make us afraid?"

"If you want," Harrison said, "you can think of it as a scheme to make *me* less afraid *for* you."

"All right then," she said. "We trust you. I shall certainly be willing to listen to you."

"What I had in mind," Harrison said, "was a legal partnership. Lawyer Frye could draw it up. Better yet, he could help make it public knowledge. You and Nevvie and I could enter into a partnership. The kind of thing where neither you nor I could lease or transfer ownership or rights without the other's consent. That way anyone who was trying to muscle the Amelia One away from you would have to come find me too or it wouldn't be legal."

Mrs. Wiggin said nothing and Harrison hastened to add, "It would be a partnership on paper only, of course. I want you to know that from the beginning. I wouldn't expect or want any of the possible income from the mine. It would still really belong to you and Nevvie. But this way no one could force you to do something with it that you didn't really want to do. Do you see what I'm saying?"

"I would have to talk it over with Nevvie, Harrison."

"Of course, ma'am."

She thought for a moment. "But I don't have any objections myself. If it would make you feel better about it."

"It would, ma'am. It really would. I know you think I'm silly with my worrying, but I would truly feel better if you would do this. And I promise you, I wouldn't be trying to take anything away from you by it.''

Mrs. Wiggin smiled and leaned down to give Harrison an almost motherly kiss on the cheek, which by now was quite bristly with beard stubble. ''That thought would never cross my mind, Harrison. Or Nevvie's.''

''Please talk it over then, ma'am.''

''Amelia,'' she corrected. ''Everyone in Goldfield knows me by Amelia.''

''Yes, ma'am.'' He grinned. ''Amelia.''

That afternoon they brought George Frye back to the cafe. The lawyer not only agreed to draw up the partnership papers, he volunteered to waive his fee for the service.

''I've been feeling guilty,'' he said, ''about opposing you when I was in the wrong.''

''Did you ever find out who your client was?'' Harrison asked.

''No, but if I do I can promise to give you the second shot at him,'' Frye said. ''Behind mine.''

CHAPTER 31

Harrison was becoming able to walk without extreme discomfort. He was able now, after a week, to go to the backhouse by himself and, thank goodness, to dress himself. Another day or two and he would have no more reason to remain in Goldfield.

He was discovering already that he was feeling pangs of regret that he had to leave. He was not looking forward to a return to Denver and to the drab day-after-day sameness of his job at the bank.

Yet if he chose to remain—for no reason whatsoever—he would be doing Mrs. Wiggin and Nevvie a disservice. And he could hardly repay them in that coin after their kindnesses.

If he lingered here he would continue to put them out, literally out of their own beds for most of this past week. Worse, he would endanger them.

The Amelia One was now legally a three-person partnership in which the signatures of any two were valueless without the third signer. But if Harrison remained in Goldfield, all of the partners would be there and would be vulnerable to any schemes this unknown California Investments, Ltd., group might assay.

Harrison could not impose that risk on two such fine women as Amelia and Nevvie Wiggin.

There was, however, a thing or two he would like to clarify before he left.

For the first time in what seemed a great while he found his coat and cap and pulled them on. He fingered his chin after he tugged the cap in place. The growth was not yet a beard but by now it was more than a stubble. At least now it looked deliberate rather than lazy. Nevvie said she liked it, although there was a sprinkling of salt-and-pepper gray beneath his mouth to match the gray at his temples.

Premature, Nevvie claimed with that light, clear ring of

bright laughter that met the ear so delightfully. Premature and distinguished.

Harrison smiled.

He turned toward the front of the cafe and was startled to see a carriage draw to a halt in front of the open flap. Carriages were rare here. The streets were full of wagons and carts of any size or description, but carriages were decidedly rare.

If he had been surprised by the appearance of a carriage, he was shocked to see who alighted from it.

Martha.

Martha Blakemon!

Here.

Harrison could hardy believe it.

It was most definitely Martha, though.

She stepped down onto the dusty Goldfield soil with all the elegance of an arrival at a Brown Palace soirée, handed the driver a coin without deigning to speak to the man and raised her chin high before she gathered up her skirts and marched inside the cafe tent.

She looked, Harrison realized, cool and lovely, even beautiful. Quite possibly one might say regal.

She was a vision, with gown, bonnet and parasol in matching shades of royal blue velvet. Her hair was faultlessly arranged, her composure assured.

No one could have been lovelier.

Harrison found himself too startled to be pleased to see her.

He stood rooted where he was for a moment.

Martha passed into the shadowy interior of the tent. She saw Harrison standing there, speechless, and came to him to take both of his hands in hers and to offer her cheek, which he dutifully bussed.

"Harrison. You've been injured. And that beard!" She made a face, then laughed gaily. "But I am *so* glad to see that you seem well enough. I was worried about you. So was Daddy. We hadn't heard a *word* from you since you left, and our letters were unanswered. So I came to be with you in this time of trial."

Letters. Harrison had never thought to call at the post

office for general delivery mail. Or possibly they had been sent to the Tonopah address, where he had spent only a single night. Regardless, he had never thought about anyone writing to him here.

Concern about the letters ran through his thoughts, giving him something to focus on while he tried to accept the fact that Martha was here.

Martha rambled on, not pausing for answers, thank goodness, telling him about her trip, telling that she and Aunt May had been forced to take *wholly* unacceptable rooms at a *revolting* hotel because there were no decent facilities available, telling him that the heat of Nevada was im*poss*ible, telling him how very *much* she had missed him.

Harrison smiled and nodded, comprehending perhaps half of what she was saying.

"And your clothing, dear. Really! Thank God I took the liberty of bringing you something acceptable. If there is a barber in this God-forsaken village you can be back to your old self before dinner, dear."

Martha cut her eyes sideways without stopping her flow of words, and Harrison was aware that Nevvie and Mrs. Wiggin had heard the arrival and come out to the front.

"Are these the people who have been tending you, Harrison? I heard all about it, you know. At the hotel. But really, dear, I do hope no word of this will reach home. People simply would not understand a single gentleman living in such an arrangement. But of course no one shall mention it ever again, I'm sure." She smiled and touched Harrison's cheek.

"I've taken a room for you at the hotel now, dear. Oh, I know you don't like to accept favors from Daddy or me. But it must be done." She reached into her handbag for her purse and asked, "What do we owe the, uh, ladies for their services, dear?" Martha's expression and tone of voice were nominally cheerful and pleasant, but there was a chill underlying them that could not have been mistaken.

"I think," Harrison said, "you are in error here, Martha." He motioned Mrs. Wiggin and Nevvie closer. "Ladies, I would like you to meet Miss Martha Blakemon.

Martha, Mrs. Amelia Wiggin and her daughter, Miss Nevvie Wiggin."

Only when the words were already out and Martha gave him a wide-eyed, cutting look did Harrison realize that he had made the blunder of introducing them in the wrong order. Martha was almost his fiancée, was admittedly his intended. He should have performed the introductions the other way around. The mistake might have gone unnoticed by two of the parties but certainly not by the third. He had done it without thinking, and now he regretted that.

"Harrison owes us nothing, Miss Blakemon," Mrs. Wiggin said with dignity. "Friends do not expect payment."

Martha's eyebrows went up.

"I'll explain everything later," Harrison said. "Everything," he promised.

"I should hope so," Martha said. Her voice and the look she gave Nevvie were barely short of being catty.

Martha turned and headed toward the carriage, which was still waiting at the front of the cafe.

Harrison had little choice but to follow. He glanced over his shoulder to give Amelia and Nevvie a look of apology, but there was nothing he could say or do to explain until he had Martha safely returned to the hotel. He hoped they would unerstand.

But they would, he thought a moment later. Of course they would.

Both of them were as kind as they were generous.

Better to talk to them later anyway, alone, so Martha would not feel offended by Harrison's need to apologize for her conduct.

That was probably something Martha would not understand if she became aware of it.

Harrison waved a quick good-bye and followed Martha to the carriage.

CHAPTER 32

For the first time in years Harrison was aware of a feeling of constriction from the high collar and tie at his throat. He had become accustomed to both over the years, but now it seemed that a few weeks of rough clothing and open collars had changed things more than he would have expected.

They ate in the hotel dining room, which Harrison thought quite nice. The pot roast was excellent, if not as tender as what Mrs. Wiggin fixed in her primitive cafe. Martha was not pleased, though. She had had her heart set on duck this evening, and the closest the hotel could come was a rich chicken and dumplings dish.

"I thought you were going to shave," she said late in what had turned out to be an almost silent meal.

"I haven't decided," Harrison said. "Personally I think I'm going to like a beard."

"I do not," Martha said pointedly.

Harrison grunted something that Martha could interpret however she wished and took another bite of the pot roast.

"You haven't told me yet about your prospects for selling the mine," Martha said.

"I, uh, don't have it."

"No prospects? No matter, Harrison. Daddy suggested you turn it over to a broker to handle for you. That way we could leave for home immediately. I talked to Daddy before I left, Harrison, and I have good reason to believe he would advance you, strictly on the basis of a business loan, the amount necessary for a partnership."

"What I meant," Harrison said, "was that I don't have the mine any longer."

"You sold it already? But why didn't you tell me?"

Harrison sighed. "I did not sell it, Martha. I gave it to

the people John J. really wanted it to go to. I gave it to Mrs. Wiggin and Nevvie.''

Martha looked shocked. "Gave?"

Harrison spent the remainder of the main course trying, without noticeable success, to explain the transfer to Martha's satisfaction.

"But what about the partnership?" she kept asking. "What about our house?"

It tried Harrison's patience, but he continued his attempts to make her understand that he did not regret for a moment the decision to transfer the Amelia One to Mrs. Wiggin and her daughter. He was relieved when during dessert George Frye passed by their table, paused to make sure Harrison really was the person he thought and then stopped beside Harrison's chair.

The lawyer smiled. "I almost didn't recognize you, Mr. Wilke."

Harrison conceded that the change in outward appearance probably was considerable, but he did not offer any explanations.

"It was a stroke of luck running into you this evening," Frye said. "Saves me a trip in the morning."

"Oh?"

"It occurred to me this afternoon that you really should have your partnership recorded at the courthouse. To ensure against pilferage of the documents, if you see what I mean."

"I have to go over there tomorrow anyway," Harrison said. "Thank you for the advice. I shall take it, sir."

"Good." Frye nodded toward Martha and tipped his hat.

"Who was that man?" Martha asked when the lawyer was gone. She seemed unwilling to concede that anyone in Goldfield might be considered a gentleman, although at home she would naturally have assumed a gentleman's status of anyone dressed as well as Frye had been.

Harrison explained.

"He mentioned a partnership to you?"

"Yes."

"Well?"

Reluctantly Harrison explained that also.

"So you still do own half the mine," Martha said with a show of some interest when he was done.

"A third," he corrected. "On paper only. I have no intention of drawing any income from the property. The partnership is nothing more than a legal device."

"Harrison Wilke! How can you be so stupid!"

He gave her a cold glare, the like of which he had never done in the past.

Obtuse though she might have been in some ways, she was uncomfortably aware of his sudden hostility now. She blanched, then quickly tried to recover with a smile and a cheery, "But of course you know what is best, Harrison."

He grunted again.

"You told that man that we are going to the courthouse in the morning. Does that mean we won't be starting for home tomorrow?"

"I said nothing about 'we,'" Harrison said coolly. "I am going to the courthouse tomorrow. Alone. *With* my beard intact, thank you. I have no idea when I shall come back to Denver." There. He had said it. If Martha did not like it, she could go back without him. In fact, he rather hoped she would. Her company was not as pleasant here as it had seemed in Denver.

"Yes, Harrison," Martha said. It came out practically as a simper, which only made it seem false, not contrite.

Harrison could not help but wonder if she had always sounded like this.

Or, heaven forbid, if *he* used to sound like Martha did now. Back when his ambitions had all been tied to financial success and social position.

He made a face and took a small bite of chocolate cream torte, wishing as he did so that he was having cherry cobbler instead.

CHAPTER 33

Harrison felt ridicuously pleased to be back at the cafe for breakfast. He had not slept well the night before. The hotel bed was comfortable enough, but he had spent much of the night lying awake worrying about how Mrs. Wiggin and Nevvie were faring. He kept thinking that the California Investments, Ltd., people might not yet know about the partnership. And if anything happened to the Wiggins and he was not there to protect them . . .

Now, though, everything was all right. They were well. They had even seemed pleased to see him this morning.

Harrison was not sure, but he thought Nevvie might suddenly be feeling shy with him. He did not think she was actually avoidng him. Exactly. But Mrs. Wiggin had come out of the kitchen to serve at the table Harrison had chosen, and Nevvie seemed especially busy this morning handling orders at the other tables.

When he was done, and most of the other customers as well, he went into the back.

"You look very handsome this morning, Harrison," Mrs. Wiggin said. Nevvie, who was nearby washing dishes, gave her mother an angry look that Harrison did not understand. Possibly the two had had a disagreement about something last evening, he decided.

"Thank you."

"You and Miss Blakemon make a very attractive couple," she said.

Harrison did not know why the compliment should make him feel uncomfortable. But it did.

"I suppose you will be leaving Goldfield soon?"

"I really don't know, ma'am." He smiled and corrected himself before she could speak. "Amelia." She smiled back at him.

"What I came to ask you," he said, "other than how

you are doing, is would you know where I could borrow a light rig of some kind.''

"You, too, Harrison?''

"Me too?''

"Oh, you and Johnny. So much alike. That's all. He never had transportation either. And he always was looking to borrow a driving rig, never a horse.''

"John J. was a terrible rider. So am I, for that matter. I can do it, but I've never liked it. John J. was the same.''

Amelia, remembering, became bright-eyed with unshed tears. She gained control of herself, wiping her eyes as she pretended to wipe her forehead with the hem of her apron, and said, "I suppose you could borrow Mr. Horst's buckboard.''

"No, Mama!''

It was the first he could remember Nevvie saying since he had arrived.

Mrs. Wiggin broke into tears completely. She turned away from the stove and ran to sit on the edge of her bed with her face buried in her apron. "I forgot,'' she wailed. "I actually forgot. I can't believe I did that. I forgot.''

"What's wrong?'' Harrison asked.

"Mama . . . I . . . you can't borrow Mr. Horst's rig, Harrison. Please.''

"Why?''

"That's the rig Johnny was driving when he had his accident. We'd be frightened half to death if you took that over the same road. The same horse. You know how they are. If they take a scare once in a place they are so apt to do it again at the same place. They don't even need a reason the second time. It would just be too frightening.''

"John J. was in a wagon when he had his accident?''

Nevvie nodded.

"I guess I'd just assumed all along that he'd been horseback that time. And of course I know what a horrid rider he was, so I just assumed . . .''

"No, he was in a wagon. In that wagon. He borrowed it that afternoon.''

"It isn't so easy to fall out of a wagon. Unless the wagon wrecked.''

"Oh, it didn't wreck. But it must have hit a rock and the jolt threw him out. Something freakish like that. It can happen, Lord knows. It did happen." Nevvie began to cry too now.

Harrison stood there awkwardly for a few minutes more, but neither of the women was paying any attention to him now and he felt uncomfortable, like an intruder. He turned and left the cafe quietly.

He had not really wanted to use Martha's hired carriage, but now he decided he should if he wanted to get to the courthouse early.

He agreed with Nevvie, though. He did not want to make that drive in the same wagon from which John J. had fallen and been killed. It just would have been too miserable a journey.

CHAPTER 34

The visit to the courthouse took a great deal of time, but not because any of it was particularly difficult. It was slow, methodical, meticulous work, going from this clerk to that, from this plat book to that office file. For someone accustomed to the extraordinary detail of banking ledger entries it was not difficult at all.

Harrison plodded from this office to that until one o'clock and took a break for lunch, then went back to the courthouse for another slow pursuit of information.

Recording the partnership document had taken him less than fifteen minutes. The rest of it had another purpose.

When he was done, shortly before the county offices closed for the evening, he was satisfied. He was also sad.

"Friends," he told the carriage driver when he finally returned to the rig Martha had reluctantly lent him.

"Sir?"

Harrison shook his head. He really did not feel like talking much at the moment.

The driver held the door for Harrison to enter the closed carriage, then stood for a moment before he closed it. He looked worried. "Miss Blakemon ain't gonna be happy about this, sir."

"About what?"

" 'Bout you takin' so long, sir. She said something this mornin' about getting back t' Tonopah in time for th' last eastbound. Too late for that, sir. Too late for sure."

"I'll explain everything to her, Lyle. If she gets mad it will be with me, not you."

The driver touched the brim of his cap. "Thank you, sir." He closed the door and climbed into the driving box to take up his lines.

Harrison smiled and reflected that so many things changed

just because of the clothes a man had on his back at a given moment.

Yesterday morning Lyle would have spat and muttered and cursed at him to avoid making Martha Blakemon unhappy. The way Harrison was dressed now, though, the man touched the brim of his cap in deference to Harrison's supposed authority.

Funny world, Harrison decided.

Almost hilarious.

For a moment he felt almost like crying.

The carriage rocked forward quickly, and Harrison was grateful for the supple suspension built into the well-made vehicle. The team was fresh and Lyle was in a hurry, and the ride would have been extremely rough without the soft springs built into the undercarriage of the rig.

Harrison wondered briefly why he was thinking about things like that.

Then he realized.

It was easier, simply easier, to think about inconsequentials than it was to think about more serious matters.

Like friendships.

And trust.

And decency.

After a while, when it was dark and he was sure no one could see, he did cry a little.

CHAPTER 35

He was buttoning his shirt when Martha knocked on the hotel room door. She must have heard him moving inside or may have seen the lamplight under his door. Certainly he had not told her that he was back. He opened the door and let her in.

"Harrison. Why on earth are you putting those filthy old things back on?"

He finished buttoning and turned around, away from her, to tuck the shirttail into his trousers.

"Harrison, I asked you a question."

"I know, Martha. I'll tell you about it later."

"You can tell me about it now, Harrison. Do you realize that you were gone all day *long?* Do you realize that now we can't possibly make the night connection east? Do you realize we have to stay here another whole *day?* Do you realize that, Harrison?"

"Of course, Martha." He smiled at her and grabbed up his old cap and coat.

"Harrison. Where are you *going?*"

"To a saloon, Martha." He started for the door.

"Harrison!"

" 'Bye, Martha. I'll talk to you later."

He walked out, leaving the door open, and hurried down the stairs and out into the night. He turned to his right, away from the cafe, toward the Golden Garter, Goldfield's largest and busiest saloon. Hot as the day had been, the night air was cool to the point of being chilly. He turned his collar up and hunched deep into his coat as he walked.

Harrison had never been inside the Golden Garter. It was not as large as he might have expected. In Denver it would have been considered a mediocre sort of place.

There were perhaps forty customers in the place, more or less equally divided between the long hardwood bar and the section set aside for faro, roulette and card play. There was sawdust on the floor, and the lights were cheap, the cuspidors made of formed tin rather than brass.

Despite the suggestion implied in the name, there were no women in the place. The Golden Garter was a place where men could come to drink and socialize and gamble. If they wanted something else they apparently had to look elsewhere.

The men were talking, drinking, relaxing. They were not loud; certainly they were not rowdy.

Harrison stopped at the door and stood there for a moment, surveying the crowd. Some of the men he recognized. He had seen them at the cafe or in the crowd at the court hearing. A few he had spoken to when he was asking questions about John J. Several of them had been among the witnesses George Frye had called against him. Others had been among those who responded the night the thugs tried to molest Mrs. Wiggin and Nevvie.

They were good men, he knew. Good, honest men. Harrison liked and respected even those of them he did not know.

He smiled. Over there at the roulette wheel was a figure he recognized, a man he did know.

Instead of approaching that man, though, Harrison went to the near end of the bar where a pair of short, dark-complected men were getting quietly drunk.

"Excuse me."

The two stopped their drinking and looked at him. It took them a moment to focus on the newcomer's face.

"We know you, bud?"

Harrison smiled and shook his head.

"You want a drink? Eh, we can buy you a drink." The drunk turned and waved toward the bartender. The motion was limp, fluid, as if his bones were melting under the influence of the liquor.

"I don't want a drink," Harrison said. "But I would like to ask you a favor."

"Yeah?" The man grinned, exposing teeth long in need of cleaning. He reached for his pocket, missed and stabbed at it again.

"Not money," Harrison said. "Is that a gun in your pocket?"

The man blinked, took his hand out of his pocket and felt the side of his drooping coat. He smiled and nodded.

"Careful, Tony," his companion warned. "Thiz fella migh' wanta shoot somebody."

"Naw, I don't wanta shoot anybody," Harrison said pleasantly. "I just want you to shoot that thing once or twice. Show me how it works."

"That's all?" the man asked.

Harrison nodded.

"Helluva favor, is what I say."

"I want to see how loud it is."

The drunk looked at his friend, shrugged and on the second attempt managed to drag a small, nickled revolver out of his coat pocket.

"Careful," Harrison said. "Don't point it at anyone."

The man seemed to find that funny. He began to giggle.

"Just down at the floor," Harrison said. "We wouldn't want to hurt anybody."

The man giggled some more. He used both hands to hold and cock the little revolver. His aim wavered, and for a frightened moment Harrison was not sure the fool could hit the floor.

The drunk pulled the trigger, and the tiny revolver fired with a huge roar.

The man laughed and fired it again. He lost his balance for a moment and lurched sideways, bumping into the bar. He dropped the revolver, and Harrison breathed a sigh of relief. A great many things had changed over the years, but Harrison was still uncomfortable around firearms.

All the noise, all the buzzing conversations in the Golden Garter had been interrupted. The customers were quiet, craning their necks to see what was happening at the end of the bar.

Harrison thanked the friendly drunks and climbed on hands and knees onto the polished surface of the bar, ignoring a yelp of protest from the bartender.

He stood upright, where everyone could see, and waved

137

his hands to make sure he had the attention of everyone in the place.

He did.

He cleared his throat and paused for a moment.

"Boys," he said, "I have something to tell you."

CHAPTER 36

"How many of you men knew John J. Trohoe?" Harrison had felt a moment of awkwardness. He had been nervous. Now he was calm. It was going to be all right.

"How many?" he repeated.

A few of the men in the crowd looked blank. Others looked toward people who were standing close to them. But at least a third of the crowd nodded or raised their hands to show that they had known John J., they did remember him. One man remembered him and had known him well enough to cry out, "Helluva good man, John Trohoe."

"Right," Harrison said to that man. "A good many of you here remember him. Those who don't need to hear about him too. Because what happened to John J. could happen to you too."

The crowd was curious now. Several of them tried to ask questions.

Harrison held his hands up, the way he had seen politicians do to quiet a group of noisy supporters, and gradually the sounds died away again.

"I want to tell you a story," Harrison said in a clear, firm voice.

"I want to tell you a story about friendship. And deceit. And theft. And even about murder."

He clearly had their attention now. The men stood or sat in place. The roulette wheel was idle. In the entire bunch only one man moved, pushing his way through the others toward Harrison.

"I want to tell you," Harrison said, "about the ways a man here in Goldfield might have his claim ripped away from him and from those he holds dear. About how even after a man's death he could be robbed and the folks he loves denied what he worked to leave them.

"About how false enterprises and false trails can be laid to cover the tracks of a thief and a murderer so that the thief can come in in broad daylight and try to take away a good man's legacy to his loved ones.

"And I want to tell you where the truth of it all lies. So you boys can go see for yourselves if I'm telling the truth or not.

"Then I want you to make up your own minds about what ought to be done with a man who'd do that kind of thing to someone who called him a friend."

Ralph Horst lunged the last few feet. He grabbed at Harrison's feet and yanked at them, spilling Harrison off the tall bar to the sawdust and cigar-butt-littered floor.

Horst began to kick Harrison's barely healing ribs.

CHAPTER 37

The Goldfield miners had Harrison propped in one chair and Ralph Horst seated—contained, really—in another. Someone had put a bottle and a glass on the table beside Harrison. Gratefully, but moving very carefuly, he helped himself to a glass of the fiery stuff.

"It's all there," Harrison was saying. "In the records in the courthouse.

"John J. filed on the Amelia One fairly late, but he was out far enough from the rest of the claims that there weren't any others around him. I guess he found some color to begin with."

"Had to," someone injected, "or they wouldn't of accepted the claim."

"Right. Well, there was some color, obviously, but it wasn't a big strike. Nothing to get anyone excited about it. Then more than a month later everything around him was filed on too." Harrison paused. "Would it be possible to fake a claim's initial findings?" he asked the man who had just spoken.

The fellow shrugged. "I expect it would. Be a lot of trouble, though. You'd have to take ore from someplace else and say it was from this new claim. Don't know why anybody would want to do that, though."

Harrison smiled. "There would be, I'll bet, if an adjacent claim had a vein on it and the new claim was trying to cut that vein."

"Couldn't work that way," the man said. "A claim covers just the surface ground. But once you find your vein, mister, you got the right to follow it wherever it leads, till you run into somebody else's tunnels underground or till the vein surfaces, whichever. Once you're underground, though, you can follow ore clear to Nebraska an' still be legal."

Harrison smiled. "That's what they told me at the courthouse today. But what would happen if the man who owned the first claim didn't know that he'd gone down past the vein and was still looking for it?"

The man looked thoughtful for a moment. "Ayuh," he said. "Be possible to cut a vein that way."

"I'm just guessing about that," Harrison said. "But I'll bet it's so.

"What happened with John J. was that he had this so-called friend working in the shaft with him. So it would have been possible for that bastard over there to have found something and not told John J. about it. But I'm still guessing about that.

"I can even guess, though, which side of the shaft he found the vein. The southeast. Because a few weeks before John J. died, Ralph Horst filed a claim on the southeast side of the Amelia One. Then he filed another on the east and then one on the south. And finally one on the northwest. I guess that was in case the vein was running the other way from where he thought it was.

"Anyway, it's pretty obvious he didn't locate anything on his own claims. Although what with still working for John J. and claiming to be his friend he wouldn't have had much time to do development work on his own property. Or maybe he just decided to do things the sure, easy way and that's why he killed John J."

Horst cursed and tried to jump Harrison again, but a dozen hands held him back.

"I know," Harrison said calmly. "I likely never will prove that you killed John J. I've thought about that, and I shall just have to accept it. But I'll tell all of you this. Anyone who knew John J., certainly anyone who knew him as well as I did, knows how strong and how quick the man was. He was snake-quick and as strong as leather. I can't imagine a bump hard enough to throw him out of a wagon without that wagon being wrecked. Off a horse, sure, but not out of a wagon where there's something solid to grab onto.

"And John J. had been down the road, too. He wasn't any pilgrim. He'd lived among hard men, men he didn't

142

know and knew he couldn't trust, nearly all his life. There wasn't any stranger who could come up close on him and do him any harm. It would take someone he thought of as a friend to do that. Someone like Ralph Horst.''

Horst snarled something but did not try to get at Harrison again.

"If you go look at the records right now," Harrison said, "you'll find that those claims around the Amelia One are owned by a bunch of different companies. Different names, anyhow. But none of those companies is registered as legal corporations.''

"You can't sell stock if the company ain't registered," someone said.

"The idea wasn't to sell stock anyway," Harrison said. "The idea was just to cover Horst's tracks.''

"Hell," someone else said, "you got to file claims in different names so they'll let you file on more'n one.''

A man standing beside him grinned and said, "Sounds like you know what you're talking about there, Byron.''

"If I do I ain't the only one in this room that does.''

"Thanks," Harrison said. "I wasn't sure about that.''

The man shrugged.

"But if you go back to the original filings on those claims, they all initially belonged to Ralph Horst. I guess the recorder or whoever knew him, so he had to put them in his own name to begin with. Then each of them would be transferred to some fake company, and he would file on another the next day. It's all there. You can check it for yourselves.''

The men were still listening. Harrison took another sip of the whiskey they had given him. The liquor was soothing, but not enough to make the pain in his ribs go away.

"One of the phony companies is called California Investments, Ltd. Which is the same phony outfit that tried to claim John J. had signed over the Amelia One just before he died. Well, that's already been disposed of in court. About all anybody really knows about that outfit is that they don't seem to exist.

"But there was something interesting that came out of that situation that I didn't really pay attention to at first.

And that had to do with the counterclaim filed against California Investments, Ltd., by Mrs. Wiggin over at the cafe. How many of you boys know her?''

Virtually all of them did. ''Hell, yes, we know Amelia. She's a fine woman, an' John would of been lucky to snare that one.''

''I agree,'' Harrison said. ''You all know Amelia.''

The ring of heads around him nodded.

''But how many of you know her first name?''

''Hell, man, it's Amelia. We all know that.''

Harrison shook his head. ''Not so. Matter of fact, when I first got here I thought her first name was Constance. Because that's the way I had heard of it in the counterclaim document. Mrs. Constance Wiggin. It was Horst there who set me straight. He said her name was Constance Amelia MacNeal Wiggin. He already knew that. So today while I was in Tonopan I looked up the lawyer who had the original paper on that counterclaim. Sure enough, it had been signed by a Mrs. Constance A. MacNeal Wiggin. So to know that Horst would have had to be the one who received service, through a messenger he sent to George Frye, on those court papers.''

''The son of a bitch,'' someone said.

''I agree,'' Harrison said.

Horst tried to muscle his way out of the chair. This time the men around him did not just hold him back, those who could reach him jabbed at him viciously with their fists, and one burly miner elbowed him in the face to put him back into the chair.

''I'd guess he was also behind that pair who attacked Mrs. Wiggin and her daughter,'' Harrison said. ''Though I won't be able to prove that either.''

''You really think he killed John?'' someone asked.

''Mister,'' Harrison said, ''when John J. and I were on the road together, I've seen a railroad bull take a swing at his head with a lead-weighted billy and never come within two feet of John J.'s skull. He was that fast. So he never was hit by any stranger. If he was hit and killed it was by a friend, someone he thought he could trust, probably some-

144

one riding right there beside him on the wagon seat. And it was Ralph Horst's wagon he was in that night."

"Siccin' Bobo and Charlie on them women, man. That ain't right," a man said. He turned toward Horst. Horst tried to cover his face but other hands held his arms down. The man smashed Horst in the face, and blood spattered onto those standing nearby.

"He said himself he can't prove none of it," Horst shrieked.

"You're right, Ralph," the miner said. "He can't prove any of it."

"You got to let me go, Bill. You got to. You can't prove it, so you got to let me go. That's the law."

The miner turned to the other men. "What do you think, boys?"

"Ayuh. That's what the law says all right," a lanky man drawled.

"If we was the law."

"If."

A ring of grinning men moved closer around Ralph Horst.

Harrison felt his stomach churn and knot. He felt no sympathy for Ralph Horst. But he knew what these men were going to do.

Neckties and belts were freely offered, and they tied Horst's hands and feet.

A group of men dirtied the bar with their boots as they climbed onto it and began to fashion a makeshift rope of leather belts that they attached to a rafter.

Willing hands lifted Horst out of the chair and up onto the bar.

Horst screamed.

Harrison closed his eyes. Then forced them open again.

No, he told himself. This time he understood. This time he realized that it was only justice that was being applied.

His hand shook slightly when he reached for the bottle that had been put beside him. But he was able to keep his eyes open. He was able to watch. He did not throw up, and he felt sure that this time there would be no nightmares.

CHAPTER 38

"Ayuh," the miner said. "We was all in here, but it was over before we knew what was up."

The deputy night marshal, a young man who was struggling without much success to grow a mustache, jotted notes on his report pad.

"He went through the crowd asking to borrow a tie or a belt, whatever."

"We all thought he was about to show us a trick or something."

"Some trick."

"Suicide, o' course. But none o' us knew it."

"Until it was too late."

"I think he was upset."

"About his friend bein' killed in that accident a while back."

"They was awful close, you know."

"Trohoe, the friend's name was."

"I think I heard him call out his friend's name just before he stepped off the bar."

"We tried to grab him, but we weren't in time."

"Broke his neck, he did."

"Pity."

"He was an awful smart fella."

Someone snickered. "Yeah, ol' Ralph, he could think up the darndest tricks."

"But I reckon he won't be pullin' no more of them."

"Deputy."

"Yes?"

"You think I could have my belt back now?"

CHAPTER 39

Harrison stood and watched while Martha's bags were loaded onto the luggage platform behind the carriage. He knew he should have been helping, but his ribs had had to be taped again and it was painful just to breathe.

"Harrison?"

"Yes, Martha."

"Your things. Where are your things?"

"Upstairs." He was going to have to get someone to carry them down for him. The pity about that, the way he saw it, was that he had practically nothing left to pay for help, and it would be a while before he could work again.

"But . . ."

"I thought it over, Martha. If the vein in that shaft is valuable enough to be worth killing over, it's too valuable to let just anybody work on it. Mrs. Wiggin and Nevvie need someone they can trust down there. It will just have to be me."

"You told me yourself, Harrison, that there may be no vein. No one has seen it. That stupid mine might be just a big hole in the ground."

He shrugged. And winced. It hurt. "I know it's a gamble, but they need me. And I owe that much to John J. He wouldn't have let me down if things had been reversed. I won't let him down now."

"Daddy won't hold your position open forever, Harrison. I wouldn't ask him to. And he certainly would not understand any more than I can how a man can give up the security and position he has to offer in exchange for"— she seemed at a loss for words—"for whatever it is you think you have to do here."

"I wouldn't ask him to hold it open, Martha."

"Would you ask me to live in these perfectly horrid, uncivilized surroundings?"

Harrison smiled with genuine mirth. "No, Martha, I could not imagine you having to live in Goldfield, Nevada."

"Don't you value security, Harrison?"

"Not half as much as I thought. Not half as much as the freedom to boom or bust."

"And . . . me?"

"You are a fine woman, Martha. A beautiful woman."

"But . . . ?"

He shook his head. He was proud of himself though. John J. would have been proud of him too. He did not feel even a twinge of sadness or regret.

"Good-bye, Martha." He took her hand and helped her up into the carriage.

She looked more confused than angry. Although, he realized, the anger would come soon enough.

Lyle got onto the driving box, and the carriage pulled away.

Harrison tipped his head back and laughed out loud.

By the time Martha Blakemon returned to Denver, Harrison Wilke would be the most insensitive ogre who ever lived, and she would be far better off to be rid of the scoundrel.

In fact, this whole thing would quite likely have been her idea. Right from the beginning.

Harrison was sure of it.

Still laughing, he turned and walked toward the cafe.

CHAPTER 40

". . . if you don't mind, that is," he finished.

Mrs. Wiggin smiled.

Nevvie's reaction was somewhat more positive. The girl squealed and ran to Harrison. She threw her arms around his neck and pulled at him so hard she lifted herself off the floor.

Light as she was, the weight was far too much. Harrison could feel jagged bone ends grate and grind against each other as broken ribs shifted. He turned pale and nearly fainted.

Nevvie's remorse was as quick as her elation had been. With her mother's help she guided Harrison back to the bed, Nevvie's bed, where he had had to spend so much time in the past week or so.

She fretted and fussed over him for several minutes until his color returned to normal and he was able to breathe comfortably again.

"Are you all right?"

He nodded.

"You'll still stay, won't you? Please say you'll still be staying with us."

"If you want me to."

"We want you to. Very much we want you to."

Harrison looked past Nevvie's shoulder to Mrs. Wiggin. He raised an eyebrow.

"We do," she affirmed. "You have the right, even if we didn't want you to. You do own a third of the Amelia One."

"I told you . . ."

"I know." She raised a hand to cut him off. "We'll talk about that some other time. I think among us we can work out what Johnny would have wanted done."

"Yes, ma'am."

"If you young people would excuse me now . . ." Mrs. Wiggin gathered her skirts and went into the front part of the cafe, although as far as Harrison could tell there was nothing that needed doing there. Everything was already done in preparation for the lunch crowd, and there had been no one in the cafe when he entered.

He looked at Nevvie, who was leaning very, very close over him.

"Are you all right, Harrison?"

"Of course."

She stroked his cheek, running her fingertips over the beard that was beginning to soften and fill now.

"I'll shave it off if you don't like it."

"But I do like it. I think you look wonderful wearing it. So distinguished." She blushed. "I shouldn't say things like that. I know I shouldn't. But it's true, Harrison. You look wonderful with a beard. Why, a man as smart as you and as good and distinguished-looking too, why, you could be or do anything. Anything at all that you really wanted. You could even go into politics like Johnny used to say you should."

Her face, so pretty he thought, was very close to his, and Harrison was beginning to feel uncomfortable again. But this time the discomfort had nothing to do with injuries or with pain. He shifted a little and drew his knees up, hoping she would not notice.

He blushed. "A politician . . . " There was a catch in his throat, and he had to pause and cough. "A politician has to have a wife to help him, you know."

"Of course," Nevvie said. "Every man should have a wife."

"I, uh . . ."

She laughed. "Aren't you over being shy, Mr. Wilke?"

He shook his head.

Very solemnly Nevvie said, "I suppose if you needed someone, to elp you with your career and everything, I suppose I could try to help."

"Are you serious?" His hand found hers. His arm slipped around her tiny waist.

She nodded.

150

Harrison pushed his head back against the pillow and howled aloud with joy and disbelief.

The noise brought Mrs. Wiggin back into the room.

"Mrs. Nevvie Wilke," Harrison breathed.

Nevvie laughed. "I shan't even have to change my initials."

Mrs. Wiggin came to stand over them. Harrison was concerned until he saw her expression.

"One thing, Mr. Wilke."

"Yes, ma'am?"

"You should treat your intended with the proper respect. I expect you to refer to her properly."

"Mrs. Nevada Wilke," Nevvie said. She giggled and bent to press her cheek against Harrison's. "Mother, can't you find something else to do?"

Amelia Wiggin tiptoed away.

Harrison turned his head and looked into Nevvie's clear, hazel eyes. He smiled.

She pressed her lips to his.

The same string of words kept repeating through his thoughts.

Nevada Wilke. Nevada Wilke. Nevada Wilke.

Nevvie kissed him, and Harrison knew that, at last, he had come home.

ABOUT THE AUTHOR

Former newspaper reporter Frank Roderus lives in Florissant, Colorado, where he raises American quarter horses and pursues his favorite hobby, researching the history of the American West. Among his other novels are LEAVING KANSAS; REACHING COLORADO; THE ORDEAL OF HOGUE BYNELL; COWBOY; OLD KYLE'S BOY; JASON EVERS, HIS OWN STORY; SHEEPHERDING MAN; and HELL CREEK CABIN.